This Fouled Anchor

Francis Woods

ISBN 979-8288-16585-6

First published 2024

This version and paperback edition printed 2025 by Kindle Direct Publishing

Copyright © 2025 by Francis Woods

The moral right of the author has been asserted.

All rights reserved

All characters, named ships and events in this publication, other than those clearly on record and in the public domain, are entirely fictitious and any resemblance to real persons or names of persons living or dead, is purely coincidental.

No part of this publication may be reproduced, stored in a retrieval system, or transmitted, in any form or any means, without prior permission in writing from the publisher, nor be otherwise circulated in any form of binding or cover other than that in which it is published and without similar condition including this condition being imposed on the subsequent purchaser.

A CIP catalogue record for this book is available from the British Library.

Front cover design by Francis Woods

Internal content and cover formatting by

Juliette Jones Editorial Services

juliette.jones.editorial@gmail.com | www.juliettejones.co.uk

Dedicated to my father, whose overalls I still wear and whose tools I still use, but whose boots I'll never fill ...

Acknowledgements

My eternal thanks go to the hundreds of thousands of servicemen and women who continue to be the backbone of the United Kingdom's ongoing commitment to deterring war and enabling peace and prosperity to rule rather than hardship, slavery and tyranny. In and amongst that exciting, frustrating, sometimes mundane but never uneventful duty … and it is a 'duty' … naval stories (or rather, 'dits' as matelots call them) become legendary and are either falsely claimed by third parties, embellished well beyond credibility, simply badly told, are clearly palpable bullshit or sometimes stand on their own merit as 'no-shit, ask-any-bastard, all-clips, FOST foulies' truths. There's not enough room to explain that final descriptor, so much to say that some dits are entirely compelling, hilarious, fearful or tragic tales which feed hungry servicemen and women's souls.

I would also like to pay homage to those at home who never live through yet have to hear these dits, sometimes over and over again – wives, husbands, girlfriends, boyfriends, partners, children, grandkids, parents, siblings, friends and secret lovers who give every matelot, pongo, crabfat, para, bootneck and reservist a reason to do what they do, that is, be part of these dits and expect you to believe every word. It's our love for you that steers our destiny.

Finally, thank you, Royal Navy.

This Fouled Anchor

Chapter One

Monday, 16 November 1981
3 November Stoker's Messdeck, *HMS Cheltenham*
0645

Everything was bathed scarlet in the hue of the messdeck's 'police lighting'. Its purpose is security but more rightly so that any number of the slumbering occupants, stacked three-high, can stagger out of their pits and go for a piss without colliding with the unforgiving fixtures or fittings in the darkened bunkspace. The whirring background noise of ventilation systems was accompanied by deep breathing and sonorous snoring punctuated by the occasional, phlegmy cough or beery fart. Thirty-one males were parked horizontally in dreamland, just as they were elsewhere in the other various messdecks on this floating man-of-war they consider their home.

Suddenly the collective calm was shattered as the ship's broadcast system crackled to life on the speakers in the compartment and the ship's Quartermaster, two decks up in the fresh Hampshire air guarding the gangway, chimed in with his Boatswain's Call, a skilful, shrill, piercing array of plips and whees designed to call the sailors to awaken. It was then followed by a flat, laconic, sneery, "Call the hands, call the hands ... c-a-a-a-a-ll the hands!" the final part delivered purposefully long and drawn out, from a man who had been awake watching the Portsmouth Dockyard slowly come to life in the winter cold and drizzle from his vantage point upstairs on the flightdeck.

In this messdeck, no-one stirred too much, however in one middle bunk however Marine Engineering Mechanic David 'Dodger' Long unzipped his sleeping bag and rolled out, and his bare feet touched the unforgiving cool lino tiles on the deck. Opposite, in a top bunk with his spotty, hairy arse-cheeks pointing outward from the top bunk, Leading Stoker Fraiser McQuinnie passed wind powerfully and almost forgivably musically and then grunted satisfactorily in his sleep almost as if to celebrate his digestive feat. Dodger slowly shook his head in disgust and proceeded in just his underpants to the mess square, the communal area where the mess's occupants socialise, drink beer and watch television. It was a basic layout and pretty much short of creature comforts but adequate for fellow MEM Adam (the Sensational) 'Alex' Harvey to sleep butt-naked, face down with his hand dipped into one of his own Patrick trainers on the deck which was brim-full of his own cold puke. Alex, who stole and used his pop star namesake's descriptor only for his own satisfaction and aggrandisement, had the skin on his back impressively nail-raked and his neck has a large, unsightly hickey.

"Alex!" said Dodger, shoving him harshly on his shoulder. Alex was unresponsive apart from deep, sighing breaths. Dodger noticed the trainer, winced and heaved a little, finding a painful swelling on the back on his head and what felt like a scab and dried blood in his hair. He tried to rouse Alex again, but with no success, then went back to his locker to find his 'dhoby-bag' and towel and went for a lengthy shit, followed by a shave and a shower.

Sunday, 15 November 1981
The Mighty Fine Public House, Portsmouth
2120

"One-sixty, darling," yelled the barmaid, over the cacophonous noise. The DJ over on the other side of the pub clumsily switched tracks and now *Bedsitter* by Soft Cell thundered in over his piss-poor, overdriven PA. Everyone shouted loud to be heard including Alex who thanked Dodger for his pint of blackcurrant flavoured snakebite, sipping an inch off the top of the purple fluid. They moved with their pints tenderly balanced like lumpen ballerinas through the jostling crowd toward the rear of the pub where the pool table and toilets were. It was slightly less frantic there and you had a better chance of connecting with members of the opposite sex transiting to readjust their makeup, gossip loudly or copiously piss in the frankly disgusting, inhumane lavatories. The pool table itself was occupied by two such ladies both amply gifted, both gaudily made up and dressed to slaughter. Neither were particularly proficient players, and they clumsily knocked the balls around, fluffing shots and cackling whilst nearby a knot of skinheads watched with gathering frustration and annoyance. The game ambled on longer than it should with no progress and one girl lined up another shot which Dodger, no player himself, could see from her alignment was set to ricochet harmlessly around the cushions. He did however get a great look down her vest top at her breasts as she bent over the scruffy blue baize. At twenty-one, Dodger's mind did the rest.

Eventually the girls made their way to the last ball and before one could line up to take the shot, one of the skinheads leant in and flicked it into a pocket finishing the match. "Game over, fucking slags!" he yelled. "Now … fuck off and let the big boys on, eh?"

The girl about to take the shot was incensed, and she rounded the table and took a swing-slap at the skinhead's face and it connected really hard. The contact could even be heard over the music and the skinhead, trying to fish ten pence pieces out from his skin-tight jeans, was taken by surprise and somewhat embarrassed. His mates laughed heartily at him, and he closed up on the girl, returning the smack but with added male power and interest right round the side of her head and face with his brawny hand. She dropped stunned, sideways to the floor with her pool buddy wading in, dragging in the rest of the skinheads, and inevitably more people just waiting for a kick-off. A small, predictable melee was developing quickly, and Alex and Dodger picked up their pints, moving away from the aggro. Dodger caught a glimpse of the stricken female and his mind flashed to his elder sister Dawn, five years since, returning home after her husband had meted out yet another drunken pasting. He parked his pint and budged through the crowd toward her, trying to get her to her feet groggily, her reddened face a mess of tears, make-up and fear. As he bent to gather her, he felt a painful crack stripe across the back of his head where someone had taken the opportunity to put their mark upon anything in the way. He fell forward across the girl which took them under the pool table and out of the way and came up on to an elbow to witness Alex join the fight. To his somewhat stunned amazement, Alex ducked in and dropped two skinheads with single, accurate, hard punches and readjusted his stance to boot another straight and accurate, right in the testicles. He then grabbed a broken pool cue, possibly the one that had striped Dodger's bleeding melon, and used the blunt end to jab a fourth approaching thug straight in the face which stopped him dead. Alex stood with the pool cue, hands out as the fight suddenly halted as if to invite any other mug to get dropped where they stood. No one wanted it. He whirled it impressively over his fist and slammed it on the pool table, grabbling Dodger to his feet, leaving the girl cowering under the table.

"C'mon, buddy … let's fucking get out of here!" he shouted, and Dodger simply followed, looking at the blood from his head on his palm.

Monday, 16 November 1981
Flightdeck, *HMS Cheltenham*
1025

Dodger stood in the grey drizzle on the flightdeck of the ship looking aft over the guardrails, smoking a somewhat bent and creased John Player Special whilst cupping it against the stiff, threatening breeze. Berthed directly behind with its angular bow pointing proudly directly at him was another Type 42 destroyer, seemingly the same as *HMS Cheltenham*. Dodger looked at her brand new clean, freshly painted lines and remembered last night's shenanigans, drawing deep on the cigarette and gratefully feeling the nicotine surge warmly in his veins. His head still throbbed and the swelling and wound pulsed angrily and a nauseous feeling of hangover welled once again. He'd puked twice already this morning and had no breakfast. Suddenly Alex appeared alongside him looking like badly rinsed shit.

"Shipmate," he said groggily, and Dodger turned to him.

"Fuck me. It's alive then? You look fucking awful. And what the fuck happened to you, by the fucking way? I ended up getting a taxi back all by myself. Last I saw you were sucking the face of that dark haired bint ..."

Alex hoarsely chucked. "Yeah mate. Posh totty mate. They all like Sensational's cock you know."

Dodger grinned. "You fucked her?" This was a rhetorical question. Of course, Alex fucked her. Alex fucked everything he saw. Dodger was envious of his success with women and often thought Alex drugged or bribed his conquests. He just seemed to 'have it', whatever that was. Some men did, and some like Dodger, didn't. Alex nodded and lit his own cigarette from the end of Dodger's and gave it back.

"Colleen ... erm ... Colleen Flower." He looked at his own cigarette packet where something was scribbled. "Nope ...

Colleen … *Fowler* is her name. Her old man is a grunter on the *Wiltshire*. Filthy as fuck she was. I'm completely fucking empty … my back is in ribbons and I have a bite mark on my ball-bag. Real teeth." Dodger wasn't after proof of that last factoid and returned his gaze aft, hopefully switching the conversation of Alex's last few hours off. "I had to clean up all that spew and ditch my trainers too," he said.

Again, Dodger feigned indifference. "You've got your fucking fleetboard exam for your hook at 1330 this afternoon."

"Yeah," said Alex, shrugging. "So?"

"You're fucking wrecked. We were only going out for a few, and you were meant to be revising. We got shitfaced and you've been up some officer's wife all night. And another thing. How the fuck did you drop those four lads in the Mighty Fine? I was well impressed."

"Oh that. Akido," croaked Alex, squinting smoke from his eyes. "Sixth Dan."

"No shit? Really?" This was the first thing Alex had said so far that Dodger actually believed.

Alex coughed the cough of a forty-a-day Olympic smoker and turned bodily to Dodger, his eyes bloodshot, his hair a tousled mess and his skin blotchy and pasty. "Do I fucking look like I do martial arts?" he said, putting his hand on Dodger's shoulder. "Do I?"

Dodger reasoned inside his head that he didn't, and he'd been had. "How the fuck are you going to sit in front of three officers and convince them you know enough about marine engineering and can lead men and wear a Leading Hand's badge on your arm?"

"Mate," said Alex, smiling. "I am a living fucking legend. I know everything. Ask me a question. I'm sensational. I'm *the* 'Alex' Harvey, right?"

"Okay," said Dodger, bottoming his cigarette and flicking it over the guardrail into the harbour.

"What's this ship, here?" He nodded at the destroyer astern, where a sailor was readjusting the halyards on the flagstaff in the wind.

"Ho-ho … Dodger, me old arse-cheek," said Alex, jettisoning his own tab-end. "That there is the *ARA Santissima Trinidad*. An Argentinian Type 42. We are training up their crew before it sails home. It's a Type 42 and the same as *Cheltenham* down to the last bolt, don't you fucking-well know? We gave them the design, and they built it. I was speaking to one of them lot yesterday on the jetty. They seem like good eggs, really. For fucking dagoes, like."

Dodger was once again, impressed at Alex's worldliness and had no reason to call bullshit.

"In fact, they taught me some Spanish. Watch this." Alex waved at the sailor on the *Santissima Trinidad's* bow. "Hola!" he yelled. "Hola … amigo!"

The sailor stopped fighting with the impressive blue and white flag and looked at the men on the Destroyer below.

"Mooo-cho, grassy-arse-o! Si! Tu es la puta enormo! Fucky-very-mucho! Adios!" The Argentine sailor shook his head and looked dismissively at Dodger and Alex and carried on. Another gust of cold winter wind blew the first warning shots of heavier rain across *Cheltenham's* flightdeck and the pair retreated forward into the hangar and down below. Dodger had no idea what Alex had said, but it sounded impressive. Maybe he should learn Spanish, one day.

Saturday, 22 May 1982
16000 feet above the South Atlantic, North of the Falkland Islands
1435

Three Argentine A4C aircraft banked and descended to starboard toward a distant landform partially shrouded in the mist and wispy Stratos clouds. Already the lead aircraft had picked up the transmissions of a Type 42 destroyer's radar on its electronic countermeasures readout and the pilot anticipated that soon big, long range Sea Dart missiles would be coming at them at twice the speed of sound from that ship. They knew this, as Argentina had Type 42s, and knew what they were all about. As they quickly lost height, he instructed the accompanying jets to split and open distance for fear that if one were hit, the impact would not damage the others. The brief was clear. Attack the escort ships of whatever shape or size with the two racks of 500lb retarded iron bombs they carried under each wing and get the fuck out of there and pray there was enough fuel in the underslung tank to get them back to Rio Gallegos airbase.

HMS *Cheltenham*, 6 miles west of Cape Dolphin
1439

Cheltenham's ship's staff had been at Action Stations since 0430 that morning and were weary. During that time three raids had attacked the beachhead in San Carlos Water further south with the Type 21 frigate *Aspide* sunk in the Falkland Sound itself warding off multiple raids. No news was made of her fate or her ships company but her still smouldering hulk threw a dense, foreboding haze into the bright sky. Earlier losses of ships to the courageous Argentine forces had shaken *Cheltenham's* crew to the core. For the best part of a fearful week, this shit had suddenly got very real now that people were actually ending up in the water and dying on sinking vessels.

"Stand to, stand to, stand to. Raid building off the starboard quarter ... raid inbound, strength three, on top sixty seconds," barked the main broadcast. This was the Commanding Officer, seated between his two specialist Warfare Lieutenant Commanders in the darkened Operations Room somewhere up forward, each giving him a running narrative and solutions toward anything posing a threat through their protective anti-flash hoods. Three targets now lit bright on the Anti-Air Warfare Officer's plot and as the ship suddenly broke speed and rounded onto a western course, its target illumination radar lit one of the contacts up.

Ten sections from this Dodger raised looked through his own anti-flash at Alex, whose eyes fearfully flashed back. They sat close by each other on the deck of a cross-passageway and were part of a twenty-strong team at the Aft Damage Control Section Base, poised ready to counter any action damage meted out if the ship fell foul to an attack. This was their third experience in five days of *Cheltenham* being directly targeted by Argentine aircraft, but it was no less fearful. Maybe this was their time, just like those other poor fuckers.

"Raid inbound … thirty seconds … engage Sea Dart!" blared the speaker above their heads.

The ship lurched as the port and starboard missile beams on the foc's'le emptied in a salvo of vicious, pyrotechnic fury.

"Splash target one … raid inbound … BRACE … BRACE … BRACE!" said the Anti-Air Warfare Officer on the broadcast and the entire ships staff hit the deck with their hands over their heads.

A mile off, the lead aircraft, now conducting a series of manoeuvres and jinks suddenly straightened and bore down on the grey vessel growing large in his small oval front windshield. In an instant the moment was right, and he lifted the nose slightly to avoid *Cheltenham's* masts and aerials and depressed the release button, shedding both rails of its six bombs. Loosed of the weight, the aircraft suddenly became unstable for a while and then climbed steadily as the pilot fought to control it. He had barely a moment of relief when a Sea Wolf missile, fired from the nearby Type 22 Frigate *HMS Crossbow* crashed through the rear of his plane and blew it to pieces.

The stick of bombs from the plane's starboard wing cleared the *Cheltenham's* fo'c'sle and landed in the icy water some fifteen metres off her starboard bow. But the port wing's payload penetrated the ship's thin steel plating in three places. Two bombs travelled through several bulkheads and detonated in the midships end of the ship destroying the ship's officers' cabins and main galley. The third carried on through the ship's Olympus Gas Turbine intakes and out of the other side before exploding on exit. The raid killed sixteen sailors, whose remains were never found and injured forty others, and the ship lost all power temporarily, slowing to a smouldering halt.

Back in the Aft Section Base everyone felt the bomb impacts and explosions. The ship shook fearfully and rattled, and everyone bounced physically off the spots they lay. Electrical cables popped, sparking from their tethers and a high-pressure seawater main burst a joint firing a furious fan of freezing water across the passageway. Everyone felt the ship settle and the ventilation wind down and the lighting sent everything into dim hues as the battery-operated automatic emergency lighting switched in. Someone over the other side of the passageway yelled desperately, "Fuckin' hell … *we're gonna fuckin' DIE!*" Everyone agreed in their heads.

The broadcast, backed up also by emergency electrical supplies, suddenly broke everyone's stunned stupor.

"Blanket search! Blanket search! Blanket search!" The AAWO's tone was ragged and fearful. It was very evident *Cheltenham* was in deep trouble. The Officer in Charge of the Aft Section Base rose to his feet, pushing a fallen metal box off him. "Come on! Fucking MOVE everyone! Blanket search! Report damage back to me A-*SAP*! MOVE! C'mon … up! Get going!"

People rose and restarted their internal engines. Smoke had propagated from somewhere and half the lighting came back on. Dodger and Alex staggered to their feet to move up the port side of the ship as was their brief, checking compartments in turn for fires and damage. Dodger felt the reassuring rumble of the propellers bite into the sea through the structure beneath his feet. At least *Cheltenham* was moving, she is currently floating and as far as he was aware she could fight so they were still in the game. He and Alex progressed forward, unclipping and reclipping watertight doors in each section as they went, looking for incidents.

Four miles away an Argentine Dagger aircraft banked out of Falkland Sound at low level, avoiding the five British Sea Harrier FRS1s circling like sharks up above with their Sidewinder AIM9L missiles. The plane was one of three sent out from San Julien airfield and the only one returning. It had unsuccessfully dropped two 1000lb bombs short of the Leander Class frigate *Hero* and almost clipped a wingtip at frighteningly low-level sweeping outward over Ajax Bay trying to escape the fusillade of small arms fire and missiles screeching past the pilot's windshield. He had felt the plane take some hits and prayed one wasn't in the belly-slung fuel tank, otherwise he was swimming home, provided this ejector seat he was sat in worked correctly. As the plane was Israeli built however, his confidence was raised, somewhat in their engineering rather than the Gauchos back at the airbase. He swung the jet away from the action and in his screen, he could see two warships … a Type 22 frigate and a Type 42 destroyer the same as the *Santissima Trinidad* on which he's conducted practice attack runs the previous month. The latter ship was turning slowly and billowing smoke from her forward superstructure. It was time to help finish her off and claim his part in its demise.

Dodger and Alex progressed three sections forward on the port side passageway which ran the length of the ship. Alex stopped briefly and leant on a railing, pulling his anti-flash nosebag down. He gasped, shaking his head and Dodger, further forward, emerging from a bathroom he'd checked wondered what was wrong with him.

"What's up mate?" he said. Alex continued shaking his head, part in shock, part in resignation.

"Fucking didn't sign up for this, pal," he said. His voice was cracked and on the verge of tears. "I'm fucking shitting myself. I really don't wanna die." He looked directly at Dodger. "It's not my fucking time."

The Dagger levelled its wings off at fifteen feet above the choppy sea and the pilot thumbed the button of his 30mm DEFA cannons, nestled in nacelles in the aircraft's structure underneath the pilot. He had a full magazine, having had no chance to fire upon invading forces in San Carlos. The safety was released, and he commenced firing, ripping two spectacular avenues of spray in the water all the way toward the oncoming warship, now beam-on in his screen.

"Raid inbound! Port side! Strength …" Abruptly, the AAWO's call over the broadcast was shut off. The passageway where Dodger and Alex stood was filled with a cacophony of deafening hammering noises, flying debris and dust. Dodger hit the floor instinctively and when he looked up, daylight filled the compartment through multiple points of light, catching the floating debris and dust. The 30mm rounds had pounded everything and anything. He could hear slurping and gasping and rose on all fours. Down at the other end of the passageway, Alex lay on his back, his right leg raised and completely severed above the knee. Dodger stumbled across to him. Alex was damaged well beyond repair, one arm blown completely off exposing his ribcage and a burbling lung whilst another abdominal wound oozed tissue, guts and blood. Alex had a wide-eyed look and fought to breathe, blood also in his mouth. Dodger gathered his broken body to him. "Mate ... *mate* ... Alex ..." he said. Alex just stared and his eyes widened, and with his remaining hand grabbed Dodger's anti-flash hood and pulled it backwards off his head, dying quickly and finally in his arms.

Chapter Two

Tuesday, 20 August 1986

Captain's Office, *HMS Emperor*, Naval School of Marine Engineering, Gosport, Hampshire

1115

The shiny blue door directly in front of Dodger swung open. "M.E.M. Long!" came an authoritative shout from within the room.

Dodger snapped to attention, resplendent in his Number One naval uniform. "Sir!" he responded loudly and marched in an awkward manner into the office. There, Captain Gordon Marsden, the commanding officer of the Marine Engineering School stood behind his impressive wooden lectern. To one side stood Dodger's worryingly young Divisional Officer Lieutenant Tim Crowley and to the other side *HMS Emperor's* Master at Arms, who Dodger didn't know the name of, nor care that much either. Captain Marsden looked foreboding, intimidating and powerful to Dodger, his shoulder boards carrying four rings of experience, authority and power. Dodger brought himself to a halt.

"Salute!" said the Master at Arms, and Dodger did so, with the Captain returning the gesture. The Master at Arms continued with his own salute, "Sir, M.E.M Long. Request to be rated Leading Marine Engineer Mechanic, brackets Mechanical, as of twenty-eight January, nineteen eighty-eight, sir."

"Thank you, Master," said Marsden. He looked down at the documents spread out on the lectern, reading and flipping pages, bringing an uncomfortable pause in the proceedings. Dodger stared straight ahead, upright and stiff to attention. Finally, he said to Crowley, "And Long has recently … finally completed his Leading Hand's course with fairly decent results, by the look of it?"

Crowley sprung to life himself and saluted the Captain. "Yes sir. A few setbacks, but he retook exams and eventually made the mark in his own way." Dodger inwardly winced at this comment. He'd failed three exams and scraped through on the re-takes. He was no Einstein but did like fixing shit. Engineers do that. Quite what calculus, parallelograms and Pythagoras had to do with him changing a cylinder head on a diesel engine or operating desalination plants to provide the ship with fresh water was a contentious issue. He found maths and science a pain in the arse but made some kind of peace with them. All he wanted was the badges and the pay now before he found himself being told what to do by people, some of who'd had already overtaken him. And he'd had quite enough of cleaning and painting. Apparently, you did less of that as a killick, so he was told.

The Captain with his head still bowed, looked up at Dodger and locked his gaze. He then continued browsing the documents. "And is there any reason why I shouldn't rate him Leading Hand this morning?"

"No sir," said Crowley. Dodger could see the Captain was reading, word-for-word a particular sheet of interest which undoubtedly detailed his mental and attitudinal decline after he returned from Operation Corporate in the Falklands three years previous. He'd fallen foul of Naval Discipline, hit the booze a bit and at one stage was slated for early discharge. His father had also died in late 1984 from pancreatic cancer and his sister divorcing her bastard of her ex-husband only to see her life and mental state collapse with her kids taken into temporary care. Life had been a bit fucking shit, to be honest.

But he'd quit the booze, straightened himself out and shown potential, at fucking long last. His successful fleetboard had led to him being selected for the Leading Hand's Career Qualifying, and the physically demanding Leadership Courses which he'd just finished last week. Now he had to request to be promoted, the final say-so being on the bloke with the rings and the power stood reading his 'comic cuts'.

"Okay," said the Captain finally, and he gathered Dodger's service record up into a loose pile. He then reached under the lectern and pulled out a Leading Hand's uniform badge, swivelling it to face Dodger. Black serge, cut into an arch shape with a carefully embroidered gold braid single anchor, twined by rope, the first insignia of real authority naval ratings own.

"This ... is what you are here for. Possibly in the past you have doubted the judgement of certain Commanding Officers in awarding this badge to their prospective Leaders. I certainly hope you give no-one the reason to question *my* judgement when I award this to you. Many people have recommended you receive this, and their credibility is at stake here. They believe that you can lead their men, and they trust you. I hope I can trust you, MEM Long. It's not just a pay rise.

This 'fouled anchor' isn't just a killick's badge. It's a lifestyle. People will look at you, listen to you and follow your example. You will now have real influence and knowledge over those below you, and they must trust you too. And you have to have the moral courage to stand up and be counted, especially when times are bad and they need you."

Captain Marsden paused, locking eyes with Dodger. "Make sure you read the duties and responsibilities of a Leading Hand before you sew on these badges. Understand them, young man. Don't you dare let me ... or the Royal Navy down. Clear?"

"Yes, sir," said Roy nervously. There was a pause.

"Rated L.M.E.M," said the Captain, finally.

"Rated L.M.E.M," repeated the Master-at-Arms. Then he barked, "Salute! Right turn! Quick march ... left-right-left-right-left-right ... "

Roy complied perfectly, marching out of the office on his way to a new existence.

Chapter Three

Monday, 12th September 1988
M1 Motorway, southbound, Northamptonshire
0245

A blue Ford Orion 1.6 Ghia rocketed under the motorway junction, kicking up a huge plume of spray in its wake. The road was fairly deserted at this time in the morning, and the car eat up the distance on the glassy surface. Driving the car was thirty-six-year-old Lieutenant Commander 'Rupe' Farncombe, with Leading Regulator Frank Fairmile in the passenger seat, his older, bearded face rumbling uncomfortably against the door window as he drifted in and out of sleep. Both were from Sacriston in County Durham and shared Farncombe's car back to the south coast, and back to their destroyer. On the rear seat was an array of belongings was topped by a Royal Navy issue beige 'Pusser's Grip' holdall with Fairmile's cap secured to it. Across the front of it in gold embroidered lettering the name 'H.M.S WARWICK' stood out.

Farncome, one of the ship's senior staffers was drifting in his concentration. He'd been driving for three hours now and the conversation with *Warwick*'s Leading Regulator Frank had dried up miles back. The car stereo was playing *'Rise to the Occasion'* by Climie Fisher at low volume and he mentally noted that perhaps the last ten miles he had been on autopilot, not really noticing his surroundings or the distance the car had covered. He reached down into the central binnacle by the gear stick to fish out his cigarettes and popped the lighter home to warm it up. Awkwardly and with one hand holding the packet he extracted a fag by the filter with his teeth, flipped the end between his lips and dropped the packet back into the binnacle just as the lighter popped back out.

Up ahead, a large articulated lorry indicated right to pull out to overtake a slow-moving tanker truck in the inside lane.

Farncome fished down for the lighter and got a small finger purchase on it, but it skipped away from him out of his grasp landing on the passenger seat by Frank's leg. Instantly it started to burn a hole in his trousers. Frank suddenly burst into life and screamed in agony and Farncome tried to locate the lighter, his own index finger contacting the searing element. He too yelped in agony, and he dropped the lighter again, this time into the footwell. Frank struggled against the seatbelt and Farncome leaned forward to retrieve the lighter, fearing it would set fire to the carpet. He and Frank frantically scrabbled around, knocking the thing out of reach in the darkness. Farncome came back up to see the back end of an articulated lorry fill his field of vision. His foot barely came off the accelerator before the Orion disappeared under the tailgate collision bar at a closing speed of fifty miles an hour, shearing the roof of the car off, decapitating him and cutting Frank completely in half at the ribcage.

Portsmouth Harbour
0930

The Type 42 destroyer *HMS Warwick* edged slowly away from her escorting tugs which had drawn her off her berth at South West Wall jetty in the Naval Base. Her two Rolls Royce Tyne gas turbine engines spooled up noisily sending a beige mist upward and the propellors started to chew into the muddy-brown water. It was raining and most available sailors of her ship's company lined the upper deck guardrails to mark her departure this morning on a six-and-a-half-month deployment to the South Atlantic, patrolling the area as a deterrent against further Argentine attack. The ship was brim full of fuel, stores, provisions and resolve, but this morning minus two key members of her crew. *Warwick* glided past other berthed vessels in the harbour who obligingly saluted her as she went past and eventually transited the harbour mouth where relatives stood in the drizzle on The Round Tower fortifications with banners saying, 'TAKE CARE DANNY!' and 'C U SOON STU!' and other such personal messages. The sailors stood, resolute but blunted. This was the last they'll see of Pompey until next year and they knew a lot can change in that amount of time.

1023

In 3 November Stoker's Messdeck, Dodger stood by his locker completely naked except for one sock, towelling the rain from his hair and skin. The bunkspace was filled with his messmates getting out of their sodden uniforms and into overalls for the days upcoming work. A burly, likeable Leading Stoker called Mick Barnes rounded into Dodger's 'gulch'.

"Dodge, mate!" he said excitedly. "Heard the news?"

"Nope," said Dodger, pulling up his boxers. "Let me see … ship fucked again? No, hang on. You're fucking pregnant, aren't you, love? Congratulations. What are you expecting? Boy or girl?" Mick was the messdeck's gossip monger. What needed to be known was always known by him, and it was invariably bullshit on toast.

"No shippers," Mick replied, a small flicker of satisfaction that this scoop was going to beat the bank. "The Jimmy's dead."

"What?" said Dodger incredulously. "The First Lieutenant? *The* Jimmy?"

Just then, Colin Parsons, a laconic, humourless and somewhat sardonic Leading Stoker passed and added, "Yeah, mate. Brown bread. Him and the killick regulator. Car smash on the M1 this morning. Took two hours to cut them out of the wreckage. They were chopped to pieces. Poor cunts." Mick looked crestfallen that Colin stolen his news bulletin, and with better detail than he had.

"You're having us on," said Dodger, now donning his dry socks.

Mick chipped in, trying to recapture the narrative. "No mate. I was just talking to Terry Fullwood … the fat, gopping Captain's steward … and he reckons the Ops Officer will take his place temporarily and a new Jimmy will be flown out by Northwood this week if they can find one. The Skipper is gutted."

"So am I," said Dodger. "I liked Rupe. Everybody did. He was a decent bloke. Wife and teenage kids. And the killick crusher's missus got over cancer last year. This is fucking shite." He pulled on his bulky blue overalls and zipped them up. "I need a brew, Mick. Has Nige put one on?" He passed Mick and Colin and made his way into the mess square area, where a giant aluminium teapot contained steaming, ready-made tea by the duty 'mess cooks' of the day, in this case a young, fresh-faced stoker Nige McDonnell, already pouring himself a cup when Dodger reached in with his own cup and intercepted the stream.

"Oi!" said Nige. "Fuck off, will you?"

"Calm down, young man," said Dodger, with humour and mock authority. "Keep your fucking place and pour my fucking tea, boy."

The mess square started to fill. 'Tanzy' Lee, a short, stocky young Stoker sat – like others – sat on the bench-like seats in his boxer shorts with his overalls rolled down to his feet on the orange covers. Others, like Leading Stokers Ian Rees and 'Atky' Atkinson sat on the floor in their overalls with their backs against the seat cushions. Nige broke away from the tea pouring duties and moved round the bar area to sit down. He was just about to lower his backside onto the seats when Harry Wilmott, the senior Leading Hand of the Mess and effectively the messdeck's 'daddy' fussily blurted out, "Oi! No overalls on the mess covers! You know the fucking rules! Roll 'em down or sit on the fuckin' floor!" Nige's backside hovered, then rose. He sat on the floor obediently still balancing his mug of tea, ignoring Harry's chiding. Dodger also chose a spot on the carpet and plonked his backside down. The mess radio was on, and the familiar *Love Theme from Romeo and Juliet* filtered out, announcing a national institution was just about to begin.

"Ho!" called Tanzy, turning round to turn up the volume. "Ho!" he continued much louder. "Shit-in it! Shut the fuck up! Shhhh! *Our Tune* ... "

The mess suddenly silenced, and Simon Bates began with great broadcaster sincerity ...

"Today's *Our Tune* is a poignant tale ... "

Nige turned to Ian Rees. "Poy-nant?"

"Yeah mate," said Ian. "To do with pigs." Nige looked puzzled but seemed satisfied with Ian's explanation. Bates continued ...

"... about a couple ... who shouldn't have really started something ... that fate would eventually take a hand in finishing." This brought murmurs, some nods and calls of "yes!" from the twenty-six sailors, listening intently. This was gonna be good.

"We're talking about ... Laura, although I've changed the names here to protect the identities of those concerned. Laura met Stuart, who was married at the time to Jill ... at a wedding of a mutual family friend. They struck it off, straight away ... and although Stuart was over twelve years older than Laura ... he knew ... it was more than just passion."

"What a *dirty* old cunt," offered Tanzy.

"Stuart was only twenty-three!" said Stevie Hepplethwaite from behind the bar area. This brought cackles from some when the joke dropped. The music washed in and out and Bates continued in his bass, avuncular tones.

"… they fell in love. Soon, Stuart found he could no longer bear the pressure of living a lie to his loving wife, and their three young children … so he moved out and took up on his own in a flat in the town."

The mess was captivated and silent, save for the sound of zippo lighters, crisp packet rustlings, a solitary fart and slurping tea.

"All was well for a while. Stuart had arranged maintenance for the children and continued seeing Laura. Great news came about when in the late summer of that year, Laura announced she was expecting Stuart's baby. They were both delighted."

"Tricked him," offered Ian, cynically. "The old dutch-door action. Seen it done too many times. My mate, right …" he was about to launch into a 'dit' but was quickly silenced.

"Well … things wore on," continued the radio speaker. "But suddenly, on Christmas Eve of that year, as the snows fell, Stuart received a call at his work from his wife asking him to reconsider the situation. He knew that the feelings he felt for Laura were complete ... but there was just something wrong ..."

"Laura had a cock," said Mick. This brought cackles and laughter which Tanzy was quick to silence again. Bates was over the Chair and round the Canal Turn with this one.

"So," he continued, "without telling Laura ... Stuart checked off work and set off to his estranged wife. He had nothing to lose ... maybe he could finally get these feelings out of his mind for good and convince his wife he was happy."

"Quick sympathy-fuck, too," said Steve, and pointed at Ian who pointed right back. Obviously, this was part of some similar event in the recent past they'd partaken in.

"... and here is where the problem lies. On his way to see his wife ... Stuart's car skidded and was involved in an accident with a lorry in the heavy snow ... and he was killed."

The mess erupted. Tea went everywhere. Everyone on their feet, cheering and whooping and punching the air.

"Yes!" screamed Tanzy. "Fucking get in!"

"Fuckin', get in there!" cackled Steve. "What a result! Christmas ... shaggin' ... babies ... a car smash ... and death.

Oh, yes!" He was genuinely elated. "I fuckin' love it when they die! Har, har, har!"

The love theme swelled again and faded as the rest of the sane, 'nice' nation of human beings reflected sorrowfully on Stuart's demise and the outcomes. Then Bates cut in, "… the song I'm playing … is a special song for both Laura…and, strangely enough … Stuart's widow, Jill … it is of course …"

"*Ridin' along in my automobile …*" added Mick.

"*Here in my car, I feel safest of all …*" chuckled Ian.

The actual tune was lost in the babble and laughter. Harry interrupted all of this.

"C'mon, you fuckers. Clear the mess. Get turned to. Fuck off back to work. Mess cooks square it all away."

"What about the pigs?" said Nige. Leading Stoker Theodore 'Atky' Atkinson, reached across the bar and smacked Nige round the head with a huge right hand more accustomed to hauling tonnes of Field Gun and Limber up and down a complex obstacle course at Earl's Court at the Royal Tournament. Nige reeled from this, spilling his tea. He refrained from remonstrating with the giant Jamaican though. Everyone in the mess feared the giant Jamaican, in fact. He was dangerously massive, impressively strong and not one to fuck with, but an absolute pussy with his 18-month-old daughter.

Dodger rose, draining his tea, which tasted rank but was good enough. He dropped his empty cup into a black bucket in the bar area and made his way to the door alongside Stevie Hepplethwaite, who was still coming down from celebrating Stuart's tragedy on the radio. "You alright, shipmate?" he said to Dodger.

"Yeah, mate," he replied. "Wonder who we are getting in place of the old Jimmy?"

Chapter Four

Wednesday, 14th September 1988
***HMS Pegasus*, School of Maritime Operations, Southwick, Portsmouth**
1107

Lieutenant Commander Partrick Fowler is sat at his rather plush desk with the handset of his phone pressed against his ear, dialling a number. Once answered, he waited for the recipient to greet and conversed "… ah … hello, Colleen? Oh, it's you, Suzannah. Please put your sister on, will you? Yes. Look, please tell her I want to talk to her, will you? It is important."

He waited for Colleen to come to the phone and picked up a 6" x 4" photograph from his desk. It showed several people mugging the shot, at a party or some other function. The two central characters were an attractive, mid-thirties, dark-haired woman, entwined with a much younger, crop-haired, blonde youth in his late teens or early twenties. His right hand on her breast, the other one lasciviously slid beneath her buttocks. They are all obviously pissed, but she is also obviously really enjoying the moment. The woman is his wife Colleen, with whom he has been married for eight years. Fowler shudders with deep seated rage. Finally, Colleen comes to the phone.

"Yes?" she said, with a resigned sigh.

"Colleen?" said Fowler. "Yes, it's me. Look. I need to talk with you. Barry Wright gave me the photo of you and this … this … kid, at what looks to be someone's houseparty. Yes. Yes. Well … I'm not at liberty to say where he got it from … suffice to say, this is the fourth time, this …isn't it? There's only a limit to my patience, Colleen." He paused, his fury staring to bubble over.

"Tell me, who is he? Is it another fucking junior rating? Last time it was that fucking Stoker. What is it, a bit of rough, you want, eh?" Colleen said nothing. If anything, Fowler could believe she was enjoying this.

"You surprise me, Colleen. You're quite happy to live the life of a Lieutenant Commander's wife, but you have a sad habit of fucking every lowlife that points his dick at you."

Colleen quietly hung up. Fowler looked at the photograph on the desk. He replaced the receiver and reached over to his desk tidy, picking out an ornamental sword envelope opener and in a swift, furious movement, stabbed down into the photograph, the blade piercing the grinning face of Colleen's ride. He picked the phone up again and dialled three numbers when suddenly Leading Writer Appleby, knock-entered the room.

"Sir. Commander wants to see you, sir," she said. "Says it's urgent. Says he's been trying to reach you, but your phone was engaged, sir."

Fowler put down the phone and rose, scooping the photo and letter opener into his top drawer. It landed on a half empty bottle of Jack Daniels. Fowler left the office and walked the short distance down the corridor to the Commander's office, knocking and entering. His boss, Commander Phillip Lewis sat at his desk, writing. Lewis looked up and smiled, but it was a forced smile. Fowler knew there was trouble here.

"Ah, hello Pat! Do come in. Sit down. Coffee?" he said.

"No thanks, Taff," said Fowler. "What's the problem?"

"Right. Okay," said Lewis, losing the bonhomie. "I won't beat about the bush. Now, I know that you and Colleen are having problems at the moment ... and that the whole thing is a bit messy ... most of the senior staffers here at the school are smelling a bit of a fucking scandal." He sat back in his chair, steepling his fingers in front of his face. He'd known and served with Fowler in the past on *HMS Wiltshire* and his wife was at university with Colleen before she dropped out, joined the Royal Navy as a Medical Assistant and went on to meet and marry Fowler. Lewis didn't want to do this, but Fowler's situation was embarrassing, and his wife was a bit of a loose cannon and any continuance of this was likely to become his own problem. He wanted Fowler out of the way and off his lawn. He'd discussed this with the career managers and the Commanding Officer of *Pegasus*. It was all set-in stone.

"What exactly are you saying, Taff?" said Fowler. His voice sounded wounded and condemned. He knew the axe was coming down on him, and it wasn't his crime.

Lewis opened his right-hand drawer and took out a sheet of A4. He placed it on the table and spun it round. Fowler didn't even look at it.

"A position has become available as Executive Officer of *Warwick*," said Lewis.

"What? In place of poor Rupe Farncombe?" Fowler's voice wobbled slightly, his world spinning into a deeper storm by the minute. This wasn't what he wanted, at all. "You're fucking joking, Taff? It's on its way down south! You don't expect me to … "

Lewis raised his hands to silence Fowler. "Pat, you know that this has not come from the likes of my pay-scale, don't you? I don't make all these decisions. They are merely passed on to me, to give to you, for God's sake! Upstairs have made their minds up on this, I'm afraid." It was bullshit. Fowler knew this. He could see the conceit and lies in Lewis's words. Lewis could have blocked this, if he wanted to. He sat back in his chair and glowered ahead, at Lewis's tie.

"Here are your orders," said Lewis, sliding the sheet toward Fowler, whose gaze didn't falter. "I've arranged everything with your appointing officer. You join *Warwick* in Gibraltar, next Monday. You've had a Type 42 before, anyway, so you should be pretty au fait with the workings. You'll get your XO's course on return, and anyway, this could be conducive to your promotion to Commander."

The last sentence was just muddy noise to Fowler. The anger and injustice in his head were thudding hard and his heart pounded harder in his chest. Someone was gonna fucking pay for this shit.

Thursday, 15th September 1988
106 Swift Avenue, Fareham, Hampshire
0315

Fowler sat alone in his lounge, a tumbler of whiskey in his right hand. He stared ahead, and has held this position for about an hour, not even moving. His cheeks were streaked with the tracks of dried tears and the inside of his mouth coppery to taste with the blood from a ragged piece of tissue inside his cheek he'd chewed and bitten. He has a note in one hand too. On the Compact Disc player Terence Trent D'Arby's *'Sign Your Name'* was playing:

"... *time I'm sure will bring, disappointments in so many things ...*"

Fowler's eyes unlocked and lowered, and he sighed, deeply. He rose and went unsteadily into the kitchen, placing the glass and note on the table. The note read:

"I really need you to know that I don't care if you are going back to sea. The sooner the better, as far as I am concerned. I don't consider you part of my life anymore. Leave me alone and fuck off out of my life. Colleen"

Fowler rubbed his eyes with the heels of his hands and sparkles filled his inner vision. He swayed slightly, went to correct himself and then fell backwards without stopping, the back of his skull smacking the edge of a work surface quite hard. He lay there for five hours, unconscious, his face twitching and ticking.

Chapter Five

Tuesday, 20th September 1988
Gibraltar
0945

British Midland flight BM128 swung round to line itself up with the runway running across Gibraltar's main thoroughfare north to the border crossing with Spain. In seat 6D, Fowler sat with his face almost a rictus mask of tension and anger. For all of this, sat next Fowler was a 22-year-old student who'd slept throughout the short flight from East Midlands Airport as she'd dropped two Xanax and a miniature gin in the ladies before boarding.

In the airport waiting bay sat *HMS Warwick's* Master-at-Arms Jim Conway in a dark blue Leyland Sherpa 'tilly' minibus with 'ROYAL NAVY' stencilled on the side but painted hastily over in the light of *Operation Flavius* seven months and the still-present threat of Irish Republican action against UK forces. With Conway was the ships

Correspondence Officer Sub Lieutenant Joe Sillence, for whom this deployment was the first time he'd been detached from the UK. He had nothing of interest to say or offer Conway, and their conversation was pretty stilted. Sillence was frankly shitting himself. He was entirely out of his depth as a naval officer and really wished he had stayed on at university and gone on to be a furniture dealer, just like his daddy. Now he'd been detailed to 'escort' and be a slave to some second-in-command of his ship and frankly he would rather be out enjoying himself drinking, sunbathing and dancing with men, of course in strictest secrecy.

Fowler emerged into the bright Mediterranean sunlight and Conway disembarked the van. His instinct told him which one of the passengers was Fowler and he approached, came briefly to attention and offered to take Fowler's case. "Sir," he said. "Welcome to Gibraltar. I'm the Joss Man." Sillence, standing behind him, smiled weakly but again offered nothing.

Fowler looked at the pair in disdain. "We're off on a bit of a trip … are we not?" he said, brusquely.

"Yes sir," said Conway. "This way to the transport, sir."

1738

Warwick butted its way through the gap in the mole breakwaters and out into Catalan Bay, turning to port and heading within UK territorial waters for the Straits. On the Bridge, Captain Stuart Belmont sat in his Commanding Officer's chair browsing documents corner clipped in a buff official file, occasionally looking up at the ship's positional situation in this busy maritime environment. Conduct of the ship itself was in the hands of Lieutenant Simeon 'Simmo' Casey, the Officer of the Watch who, along with his assistant, flitted between the centre mounted compass binnacle taking triangulation fixes, the navigation radar scope and his chart on the table at the rear. He had this down to the square metre and was good at this stuff. The atmosphere was professionally quiet save for his instructions to Leading Physical Trainer Phil Sewell, sat to the left of him with both hands on the small yoke that controls the steering gear and rudder, beside him the two levers which also controlled the ship's speed via the gas turbine engines way back aft in their machinery spaces.

"QM, set levers four zero, steer two-zero-five", said Casey, now alongside the Captain.

"Set levers four-zero, course to steer two-zero-five, sir," repeated Sewell and moved the yoke, watching the compass repeater track across the 200 degrees bearing. Alongside him, his young assistant, Boatswain's Mate Able Seaman 'Buck' Rodgers moved the port and starboard Propulsion Control Levers to forty. Casey used the helm to stabilise the ship on the demanded course.

"Levers set, four-zero. Steering course two-zero-five, sir!" called Sewell.

"Log speed?" asked Casey, binoculars to his eyes.

"Log speed, ten-point-five knots, sir."

"Very good." Casey knew he had simultaneous items he needed to concentrate and time to the second coming up. He'd spent last night planning this leaving harbour evolution, running it past the more senior Navigating Officer and remaining ever aware of changing situations around his warship. At the rear of the Bridge stood Fowler, now in his naval officer's day uniform, watching every move. Last week he was the Officer in Charge of the Navigating Courses at *Pegasus* which taught this stuff. Now he was Executive Officer of some shitbox, damned, fucking canteen boat full of cunts heading on a trip to nowhere but penguins, inbreds and seal shit.

"Officer of the Watch," said the Captain, seemingly laconic but knowing every move of this game. "This Polish bulk freighter, bearing red two-five?"

"Roger, sir," responded Casey, indicating he'd seen it and was working on a solution. It was all the Captain needed to know, save for him taking control himself and saving the ship from collision. Casey went to check his position on the chart when Fowler leaned forward.

"Officer of the Watch. Your Bo's'un's Mate. What is his name?"

Casey was taken aback. "Sorry … sir?" he said, his train of thought intercepted at a key moment.

"Your Bo's'un's Mate. The AB on the throttles."

"Yes sir. What … sir?" Casey was trying hard to get his brain back in the game and was being hassled by this strange two-and-a-half whom he'd yet to meet.

"His name, god-dammit. What is his name?" hissed Fowler. The Second Officer of the Watch looked up from the chart in surprise.

"Um ... Able Seaman ... erm ... Rodgers ... yes ... Rodgers. Sir." Now Casey's brain was disengaged completely. This ship had covered a hundred and fifty metres during this conversation, and it was approaching a programmed course change, which would put *Warwick* and the Polish vessel on opening bearings and zero risk of collision. Fowler knew this and engaged Casey's gaze malevolently.

"Get his fucking hair cut, before I stand on the fucking thing. Yes?" Casey looked back in stunned silence. Was he taking the piss, or what?

"Officer of the Watch," offered his assistant in lower tones. "One cable to course change."

Fowler gestured to Casey. "Well? Carry on."

Casey was still mentally done. He turned, just as the Captain looked across at him in a more annoyed manner and pointed at the Polish freighter using the buff folder. "Officer of the Watch ... move this fucking warship ... right now," he said.

"Roger, sir," responded Casey, still mentally throbbing from the episode with Fowler, who had quietly slipped out of the Bridge and back aft to his cabin.

Chapter Six

Saturday, 25th September 1988
Twenty miles north-west of Dakar, Senegal
1005

Uckers looks identical to Ludo and it's played a bit like Ludo. It has broadly the same rules and uses dice, counters, the same board layout and colourings. But Uckers is a Naval game, played competitively in messdecks for well over a century. The strategies have been honed by clever minds in darkened gulches late at night over hundreds of thousands of tins of beer. You learn from simple humiliation and failure. You take 'eight-piece-dickings' where none of your counters make it home and eventually you get to recognise the moment when your opponent fucks up or a throw of a dice changes the game in your favour. You then pounce and destroy them without mercy. You learn when pairings during a four-player game hobble you badly or who the players are in your messdeck not to take on when they say the clarion call, 'Uckers, you fuckers?' and they pull out the carefully hand-built playing area from its stowage and a beaker which contains the sawn-off broom-handle counters and dice. It is seen as ungentlemanly to decline a challenge and your learning process would begin. But it was and still is, a great gladiatorial spectator and contributor sport. Money, beer and teeth have been lost whilst playing it.

In 3N mess square, experienced Leading Hands Ian Rees and Steve Hepplethwaite were wrapping up an eight-piece-dicking of comparative novices MEM Tanzy Lee and Junior MEM Nige O'Connell. The game had lasted barely fifteen minutes and was like watching the 1970s Brazilian World Cup soccer Galactico masters play a pub team from Shropshire. Just two of Tanzy's blue counters were 'out' and Nige's one counter was stuck behind a 'blob' of carefully and strategically placed counters on Steve's 'doorstep'. No matter what they did, they couldn't shake sixes to break out and make a mark whilst Ian and Steve threw them seemingly with abandon and cackled like witches with every turn. The gathering crowd were also winding up on Tanzy and Nige's joint misery with glib asides and sarcastic witticisms, accompanied by 'table talk', which is meant to be helpful advice from the crowd but is nothing of the sort. Steve picked up the dice and threw two sixes and bounced two of his counters straight home. Another throw gave him a four-two, which artfully got the remaining counter home.

"Ha-ha, you cunts! Done!" he yelled, flicking V signs right in the morose faces of the younger two and sitting back, brushing his hands.

"Fucking numbers-throwing, timber-shifting bastard," said Tanzy, glumly. He snatched up the dice, blew on them and threw. Two-one.

"Steam them bits, white-boy!" shouted Atky, laughing heartily and slapping Tanzy round the back of the head. Tanzy ignored this and angrily tapped one counter forward three pitiful squares. Ian Rees picked up the dice and stood up, flicking his arms so his sleeves rolled up a bit.

"And now, ladies and gentlemen, pray silence for Professor Ian Rees, Bar, Scar and Jubilee Clip."

"… and arsehole bandit ambassador to the United Nations," chipped in Atky, his flawless toothy smile shining out from his almost-black skin. Ian frowned mischievously at him but continued to shake the dice loosely between his cupped hands.

"If you don't mind ... Mister Atkinson ... please observe." Ian tossed the dice onto the table. Six-six. He tapped one counter round up the 'pipe'.

"*For fuck's sake,*" groaned Nige and Tanzy simultaneously.

"Told you not to play him," said Harry Wilmott, casually. "Told you he's a timber-shifting, six-throwing shithead."

Smiling glibly, Ian ignored this and took up the dice. He needed a four-two to land his counters home and end the game. Tanzy raised one hand under one corner of the board, out of sight of everyone. "Is everyone ready?" he said and faced Tanzy and Nige. "You two wankers, ready?" and he threw the two blue cubes onto the board. One immediately showed a two, upwards ... and the other rolled and was about to settle showing a four to the gathering roars from the spectators when Tanzy flipped the entire table upwards sending counters and dice everywhere to deny Ian his moment. He then leapt across the table at Ian, and Nige joined in, followed by Steve, then several others, and finally Atky leapt upwards, bringing his solid, muscular frame downwards on the summit of the body pile bringing grunts and howls of pain. Atky followed it up with some robust thumps to backs, shoulders and kidneys. Harry picked up his mug of coffee and tried to ease away as the melee slithered sideways onto the carpet of the mess square.

"Oi!" yelled Harry, fussily. "Pack it in, you childish cunts!"

"Leave it, Harry!" said Dodger. "This is better than the fucking game, anyway!" He tossed the dregs of his teacup on the bodypile.

With the wrestling still going, Dodger stepped round the writhing mass with Tanzy now holding Ian in a headlock, ignoring Atky now kneeing him in the ribs. Dodger sat down next to Mick Barnes, trying to read a book and ignore the chaos. Mick made room and took out his cigarettes, offering one to Dodger.

"Nope," he said, flatly and resolutely. "You know I've given up. Go smoke it over there, you smelly fucking bastard."

Mick wasn't being kind. Grinning, he slowly drew an Embassy out of the packet and showed it to Dodger, right in his face. "C'mon, shipmate. You're one of us. You know you want one. I have you under my power..."

"Going ashore later?" said Dodger, trying to deflect Mick away from his tempting offer.

"Fucking mooch, baby. What time is leave gonna be?"

"No idea," mused Dodger. "Alongside at twelve. Can't see them letting us go before two. We're all back on board for seven, though."

"Suicide leave?" interjected Atky, who was disengaging from the playfight having punched enough people. Others were getting untangled on the scruffy carpeted area, breathless and sweaty. Underneath it all was Tanzy, holding his nose as Atky had 'accidentally' connected.

"Yeah mate. But enough time to get fundamentally cunted," said Dodger, pointing in principle, to reinforce the point.

"Damned right!" chipped in Nige. "My brother says there's meant to be this fucking cracking beach bar …"

"Great!" clapped Mick. "That's it then. Who's going with me? Stevie? Tanz? Tanz?"

Tanzy laid supine, still cupping his nose. That connection brought tears and blood to the young Stoker.

"You're going whoring it, Michael," said Dodger. "You always do." Mick just smiled wickedly and flicked an eyebrow.

"You're a fucking fanny-rat," added Steve. Then to everyone, "He was like that in Amsterdam. Couldn't keep it in his kecks."

"If your missus found out," proselytised Harry. "You've got kids, an' all ..." Harry had the habit of being 'messdeck mum, dad and parish priest'. It was well-meant but badly received at times. He was older and wiser than many, but thin rumours had it he'd spent time on 'Z Wards' at the Royal Naval Hospital at Haslar, drying out a drink problem. That was the reason to some he remained teetotal, drank coffee and tea and was in fact a bit of a bellend at times.

"Yeah, well ... she won't, will she?" Mick shot back, dismissively and petulantly. "Anyway, you fuckers can talk. Dodger, you're trapping that fit lass with the big tits up home, aren't you? You bagged off in Amsterdam with that whore."

"Erm," interjected Dodger, defensively. "It was a wank, mate!"

"Stevie," continued Mick. "You'll fuck anything with two legs and four lips. Nige ... well, you're still a fucking virgin, aren't you?"

Nige looked sheepish. He was still a virgin but didn't revel in it.

"Dodge and Stevie aren't married, Mick. You are, you daft cunt," said Harry, once again getting the inside track on morality.

"I wouldn't fuck one of those slop-donkeys you'll be up tonight, anyway," said Steve. "they're fucking riddled ..."

"I'll be alright," said Mick, nonchalantly drawing on his cigarette. "All this AIDS shit is bollocks. It's only arse-bandits and smack heads getting it anyway."

"Yeah?" said Tanzy, finally recovered but still nursing his nose. "Your tadger will fucking drop off. You'll be pissing glass." This statement was joined by widespread barracking of Mick's peccadilloes just for the sake of giving him shit. Mick invited this most of the time but smiled and waved the comments away. His dick was almost hardening in his overalls at the thought of where he'll be later that afternoon, possibly wearing two condoms despite his earlier reassuring statements on the danger of lethal pansexually transmitted infections. Suddenly the main broadcast cut in. It was Fowler.

"D'you hear there. First Lieutenant speaking!"

"Ho!" yelled Harry Wilmott, again, fussily. "Shit-in-it! Listen!" Everyone was expecting great news that as soon as the gangway was down, and they'd all be piling into taxis, in a beach bar within twenty minutes and drunk as fuck within three fast, rumbunctious hours. Or in Mick's case, nuts deep in his third prostitute.

Fowler clicked in on the broadcast again, "I've been closely monitoring the condition and cleanliness of the ship since we left Gibraltar earlier this week and I must say that I'm not impressed with the standard of husbandry. Therefore, we will secure at sixteen hundred today, instead of the advertised twelve hundred. Leave, except for exceptional circumstances, is cancelled in Dakar. We will still sail as promulgated at twenty hundred. That is all."

The broadcast clicked abruptly off, and Stokers mess stared at each other in disbelief, as if by some dint of science, every person's brains had been replaced with those of infants.

"For fuck's sake!" yelled Tanzy, angrily throwing a three-week-old copy of the Daily Star on the mess seats. Everyone's gaze rounded slowly on Harry, as if he had all the answers. It was of course, all his fault because … whatever.

"I don't believe it! I'm an exceptional fucking circumstance! I need a fucking shag!" said Mick, half in humour, half in heartbreak, entirely in truth.

Just then, Jumper Crossley, an angry young Stoker even at the best of times stomped in from the bunk-space in flip flops and a towel, but with his trademark DA barnet slicked into place. "Did you hear that? Eh?" he said, pointing roughly at the mess-deck speaker with his fat thumb. "We've been fucking digging out blind for fucking days now! We need our fucking leave. It's our fucking right to have it, you know? I'm fucking telling you!" Jumper used the word 'fucking' a lot, usually in most sentences like punctuation. His Wearside accent made it sound like 'fooken'.

Ian Ress cut in sagely, lighting an Embassy cigarette with his *'HMS Warwick'* Zippo lighter. "I reckon he's trying to make his mark in front of the skipper."

"Well, he'd better fucking sort his shit out," Jumper retorted. "I'm going to see the fucking Chief Stoker about this. He's not fucking getting away with this. Tell you what. The fucking hatches will be down if he carries on with this. I'm not fucking standing for it. Telling you. Not me!"

This brought wry smiles from the more senior members of the mess. Harry stood up, dotted out his cigarette in the top of an empty Coke can and stretched. "Yeah, sure, Jumper! You're the biggest lower-deck lawyer going. You're full of shit, mate."

Jumper was incensed. "Yeah? He'd better sort his fucking shit out before we go down fucking south, Harry. I can't see the fucking skipper putting up with this fucking bollocks for long."

Saturday, 25th September 1988
At sea near Dakar, Senegal
1735

Dodger and Nige stood at the extreme rear of the ship on the flightdeck, staring aft toward Cap Manuel, dusty pink and orange in the setting sun's haze. They were sober and dressed in overalls having been carrying out extra cleaning duties in the bathrooms below, instead of speeding back to the ship and hoping they'd make the leave curfew, full of beer and carrying shit, cheap trinkets. Only a few of their fellow shipmates had managed to put their feet on African soil, only then on official duties to and from the British Embassy in Senegal and to take gash ashore. Down below, there were many, many pissed-off sailors who'd spent the afternoon like Dodger and Nige, cleaning once again, instead of getting shitfaced and laid which was, and still is, many sailors' favourite past-time.

"Well, there goes Africa, shipmate," said Dodger. "Cultural run ashore, wasn't it, kid?"

Nige looked sideways at Dodger, unsmiling. "Would have been my first time ashore outside Europe, Dodge. I've only been to Gib. I was hoping to send me nan a postcard from Africa. Me mum will be worried if I don't send one now." There was a short pause, and Nige drew long on his cigarette. "What do you reckon to this new Jimmy, Dodge?"

"I think he's a bit of a wanker, Nige. He's obviously had a tough time in the past and now we are getting the shit for it. Maybe he was abused as a kid, or summat."

"You think he'll be like this all deployment? Six months?" Nige sounded scared, worried and somewhat resigned. He was just a boy and wasn't one who took well to pressure, this Dodger knew.

"Can't see him changing much. Once a twat, always a twat. Surprised the skipper hasn't hauled him in a bit ..."

"You two!" came a bellow, from behind them. Both Dodger and Nige wheeled round, only to see Fowler advancing on them across the flightdeck, dressed smartly in his tropical white uniform. In a fit of automatic panic, Nige flicked his cigarette over the guardrail into the Atlantic Ocean.

"Don't ditch your fucking tab-end over the side, you cretin!" said Fowler, angrily. "And what are you doing smoking in close proximity to a fully fuelled helicopter, anyway?" Fowler pointed at the open hangar where the WAFUs were busily stowing the ship's Lynx aircraft.

Dodger was transfixed. "... sir ... I ... erm ... we ..."

"Silence, Leading Hand! I'm talking to this man!" Fowler was now upon them and jabbed Nige in the chest. "What are the pair of you doing still in your scruffy overalls, too? You should both be in night clothing, like me! Get below and get changed. You will both report to me in your messdeck when

I do Evening Rounds later having showered and changed into the correct rig. Understand?"

Nige began, "Sir, we've been cleaning the ..." but Dodger moved his boot sideways to kick Nige's own boot to silence him. No explanation would be good enough and it was not worth explaining, so just take the bollocking. "Yes, sir," Dodger said, obediently. "Clean into night clothing, sir."

Fowler paused, glaring at the two overall-clad Stokers. "Right! Away you go," he hissed. "And don't let our paths cross again."

Dodger and Nige quickly trotted across to the hatch leading down to the quarterdeck and out of sight.

1915

In the Stokers' mess ten or so people were sat playing cards or watching a video on the small mess television. Tonight, it was a tape-to-tape copy of *Top Gun*, which had the last ten minutes taped over with an episode of last year's *Beadle's About*. No one was really watching it, but it's been played so many times, even those playing crib at one of the tables are unconsciously mouthing the lines.

Outside in the messdeck lobby, Tanzy Lee stood dressed in tropical uniform with his cap on, waiting for Fowler to appear down the ladder so he could report the messdeck ready for his rounds and inspection. Usually this is a formality. Yes, the mess should be clean and tidy – that's the whole point – but one of the grown-ups has to go round the great unwashed's slums once a day just to show face. That face today was Fowler himself, accompanied by the Master-at-Arms and the Duty Petty Officer. In front of this party was the off-watch Boatswain's Mate, clearing the way or bringing people to attention with a single blast on his Call. This he did as he descended 3 November's ladder into the lobby to announce the arrival of the rounds party.

"'Ten-shun for rounds!" called Tanzy through the open door to the mess square. The occupants silenced the television and stood up. Dodger and Nige were on the first two seats, clean and in tropics themselves, ready to report to Fowler.

Fowler descended and faced Tanzy, who snapped to attention, saluted smartly and announced, "Three November messdeck, ready for Evening Rounds, sir. M.E.M Lee reporting."

"Very good," said Fowler, tersely, without smiling. Tanzy led the way into the mess square. Immediately, Fowler's eye's struck upon the two reprobates he'd met earlier on the flightdeck. "Ah. Leading Hand. Your name?"

"Long, sir," said Dodger, straightening his posture. Annoying this bastard by appearing flippant wasn't going to make life sweet. The idea was to restore the balance and get out of his way and become wallpaper. Fowler however wasn't finished.

"Long, Sir?" he said, mimicking Dodger's response, turning to the rest of the Stokers. "Mmmmm! And, indeed, the rest of the Clankies. All dressed in the correct clothing for the time of day, I see. How nice." Fowler malevolently paced slowly in front of the individuals before him. He could sense their bewilderment, tinged with fear. How enjoyable that was.

"Let it be known, Stokers, that Leader Long, here, has unwittingly brought the spotlight to bear on all of you here in this mess. So much so, that," he said, turning to Master-at-Arms, "… I think we will have a quick search of the kit lockers next door in the locker space. Let's go. All of you. Open your lockers."

There was a stunned silence. Mick Barnes looked across at Ian Rees, who in turn looked at Dodger.

"Come on!" ripped Fowler. To Mick and Ian, "You two. You're first ..."

Again, nobody moved. There was an expectation that Fowler was somehow joking about this. Even the Master-at-Armed looked baffled and the Duty Petty Officer was frozen in his stance.

"*MOVE!*" bellowed Fowler, and Mick sprung to life, eagerly fishing his keys from his pocket. They all filed out of the mess square in silence, Dodger and Nige following. As they get into the bunk space, they passed a middle bunkbed where a man was cocooned in his sleeping bag, fast asleep. Fowler stopped.

"Get him up!" he hissed to Ian Rees, who shook the slumbering body. "I want his locker opened next ..."

From the bag comes a muffled and severely pissed off, "... wha ... look! Will you ... fuck off, eh? I'm on watch at midnight! Fuck off, you cunt!" It was Jumper Crossley, and his head appeared over the brim. Fowler closed right in. "Get … out … of … bed. NOW!"

Jumper slid sideways, still in the bag and onto the deck. The bag fell down off him, and he was naked, wearily rubbing his eyes, sporting an impressive semi.

Fowler was unfazed. "Don't ever tell me to fuck off again, sonny! I'll have you up before the Old Man on a charge of insubordination!" Jumper blinked and tried to stifle a yawn.

"And don't fucking yawn at me! That is contempt! Master?"

The Master-at-Arms stepped forward, "Yes sir?"

"Get this man trooped. I will see you lose a lot of leave and pay for this." Fowler angrily turned to Mick. "You. Where's the Leading Hand of this fucking messdeck?"

"Um, up on watch in the Machinery Control Room. Sir." Mick realised his error and quickly corrected if before he too was nailed.

"Okay," said Fowler. "Leader Long?"

Dodger looked up. "Yes sir?"

"You can be responsible for what I find doing this search. Let's go. Your locker first …"

Thursday, 29th September 1988
Ascension Island
0940

HMS Warwick was roped tightly to the light commercial fuel tanker *mv British Avon* about a hundred and fifty yards off the rocky coast of this mid-Atlantic-volcano-turned-intensely-busy-military-airbase. Both ships rolled long and uneasily against each other separated by two vast, black Yokohama fenders which gave off agonising squeals and roars with each movement. Every half hour or so a large aircraft, jet-powered or other would land or noisily depart from the runway above them for either the Falkland Islands or the United Kingdom carrying personnel or stores to and from the homeland. Size for size, this black mountain peak sticking out of the ocean was vying with many for the title of 'Busiest Airport in the World'. Below in the After Engine Room, Jumper Crossley stared up at the lights on the after fuelling station telling him his set of odd-shaped tanks set deep into the streamlined hull of the ship were filling rapidly one-by-one with distillate marine diesel and soon it would be time to signal those above for the tanker to stop pumping. Seven decks above and further forward in the relatively plush surroundings of the Wardroom, Lt Cdr Fowler is holding an ad hoc meeting with the MEO, Chief Stoker 'Bagsy' Baker and the Supply Officer, Lt Cdr Mitchell Braham. Also in attendance is Lt Cdr 'Buck' Taylor, the ship's doctor.

"The Captain is currently turned in his bunk and is unwell …" announced Fowler, in a matter-of-fact manner. "That's right, isn't it, doc?"

"…er, well," said Taylor officiously. "…not too good, First Lieutenant. Quite poorly, in fact."

"Will we have to get him off here?" enquired Baker, sounding concerned.

"Well, I hope not, Chief Stoker," responded Fowler, suddenly all charm and sincerity. "Right!" he called out, changing personality to motivation-mode. "Back to business. Today's plan – we will sail on completion of fuelling, not at eighteen hundred as promulgated."

The rest of the assembled personnel exchanged surprised looks, Baker raising his eyebrows on his expansive forehead.

"So … I take it you're granting no leave to the men, sir?" questioned Braham, gently.

"Certainly not, Supply Officer. Shore leave, at a place like this, is a privilege, not a right. In any case, with the frame of mind that the ship's company are in, I can hardly afford to have drunken riots and arrests to deal with. Ascension is a peaceful place and not for the likes of this lot." Fowler fixed Braham's gaze authoritatively. "No, they can wait for the glories of the Falklands." There was a short pause as Braham struggled with his inner doubts and misgivings. This man was a real cunt, and he probably knew it, too.

"They haven't been ashore since Gibraltar," he said gently, his voice lowering.

"We'll take this outside the meeting, if you don't mind, Supply Officer." Fowler scanned everyone else. "Does anyone have any further questions?" There were none. Just blank expressions.

"Good! Now, if you'll all excuse me …" Fowler moved toward the door then suddenly wheeled round, "… I'll be either on the Bridge or in my cabin if anyone wants me. Chief Stoker, fuelling report to the Navigator, as soon as you are ready. Someone get the Ops Officer to my cabin please at ten thirty, sharp. Good day, gentlemen."

1335

Dodger plonked himself on the carpeted mess square deck between Mick and Harry, in doing so the tea in his cup sloshed over the brim and scalded his fingers a bit. He reached across into Harry's lap and carefully removed a McVitie's Chocolate Digestive from the packet while Harry was busy boring a Stoker to his right with a tremendously interesting story about his fish tank at home. Dodger was entirely successful. The biscuit was removed, half sunk in his tea and squeezed into his mouth entirely before Harry turned back. Nige noticed from across the mess square, lowered his head and chuckled. Dodger flicked his eyebrows and ground up the biscuit, washing it down with a gobful of rank-tasting tea, flavoured with sour long-life milk.

"… so, the first time we are going to get ashore is on the fucking Falklands, eh? Splendid!" he commented, expecting someone to pick it up. Colin Parsons obliged.

"'Course, back in '82 on the *Suffolk* down south we were on board continuously for ninety-eight days. Non-stop. Straight-up. No-shit!" His narrative was dramatic, but stale. Fact was *HMS Suffolk* was late to the battle and arrived a week before the cease-fire on 14 June 1982, avoiding any real contact with the Argentine air-force.

Dodger was suddenly irritated. "Fuck's sake. Don't go on about that, eh?"

"Why?" retorted Colin. "What's it to you, fuckface?"

Dodger went serious. "'Cos I was on the *Cheltenham*, okay? I was caught up in all the shit on there. You fucking weren't. You can ram your ninety days up your pipe. Luxury, as far as I'm concerned."

"Ninety-eight days, actually ... and ..."

Harry cut him off, sensing Dodger's ire. "... whatever, Colin. Shut the fuck up, okay?"

Colin pulled a face and sipped his own tea. Just then, the mess square door burst open and in stepped Tanzy, carrying bundles of mail, envelopes and parcels. There was a general whoop of joy, and he staggered across to the nearest bench seat and dumped the lot, getting quickly clear of the feeding frenzy. He'd also got four envelopes of his own held in his mouth, so fuck everyone else. Mick leapt up, first to the pile and tried to play mailman.

Across the gap he'd left, Atky turned to Dodger, "D'you know something, Dodge? I bet there's fuck all for me. I think my mum and dad and my bird have forgotten all about me, shipmate." Dodger folded his arms and raised his eyebrows. He'd met Atky's girlfriend and little girl at last year's Families Day and she was gorgeous, the spit double of Janet Jackson, the pair of them sporting the cutest child he thought he'd ever see.

Mick, playing mailman fished through the pile, pulling out an envelope and reading the front. "Atky!" he called across the mess square.

Atky's head snapped round. "Yeah?" he said, expectantly.

"This one ..." said Mick, smiling, "... isn't for you, my old mate. It's for Harry." He passed the envelope to Harry and read another. "Atky!"

Again, Atky responded expectantly. Mick skimmed the letter across. As it was airborne, he added, "Pass that to Dodger, will you?"

Atky simply let the letter bounce off him. "Fucking twat," he said, the anger building.

Mick leafed further in the pile and pulled out another. "Atky!" he yelled. "Look!"

Atky was still in a bit of a mood but looked up anyway. Mick turned the envelope round and held it out, knowing

Atky couldn't read the address on the front from where he was. Atky got up, crossed the mess square and just when within range Mick proclaimed, "It's ... for ... ME!"

Atky completely lost it and dived on the cackling mailman, both grappling to the floor. He wrenched the envelope from Mick's hand and tore it to bits. Others joined in just to get a few punches in, mainly on Mick, others sat oblivious, reading their mail. Morale was suddenly a bit nose-up considering what had happened in the past few hours. Dodger rose and thumbed the pile, drawing out two more letters. He then bypassed the scrap on the floor, going through into the serenity and privacy of the bunk-space next door. Once by his own bunk he broke open the first envelope, quickly reading the contents, a notepad page of text. He held up four ten-pound notes.

"Mum," he said to himself. "You're a fucking star." He was broke and was undergoing embarrassing restrictions on board because of returned cheques he'd cashed through the ship's system and had four pounds actually on him to live off as well as a maxed-out overdraft. He then opened the other letter, fishing out two photographs showing a pretty, dark-haired girl in her twenties in leather trousers, sunglasses and a white t-shirt astride her Kawasaki GPZ900R, smiling at the camera. He flipped one over. It said:

Please take care, my baby.

Missing you so much.

Love, as always,

Louise xxxx

Mick Barnes passed noisily behind him, sweating from the exertions of the scuffle with Atky. He looked over Dodger's shoulder at the photo in his hand.

"Aw, man! Fuck me! She'd fucking get it! Is that your pash? Oh, aye, she'd get it! Nice tits! Bet she's a right fucking goer." Dodger ignored him and said nothing. He just stared longingly at Louise and wished he was anywhere else than right here, right now and preferably naked with her in bed, eating pizza and laughing at the stuff they both laughed at.

"Going on watch, Dodger?" Mick enthused, briefly checking his spotty face in the shaving mirror at the end of the gulch.

This Fouled Anchor

"Yeah man, let's go," said Dodger. He folded his mail haul up and stuffed them in his overalls top pocket.

Chapter Seven

Saturday, 26th September 1988

2014

Fowler emerged from his cabin in the Wardroom Flat, just as Lt Cdr Justin Smith-Howlett, the Marine Engineering Officer was passing. Smith-Howlett, known throughout the Royal Navy Engineering fraternity as 'Ess-Aitch' was a widely respected, silvering and senior naval officer who'd risen from the lower deck and was on his last trip in the Royal Navy before retiring on his return, early next March.

"MEO?" said Fowler, stopping SH in his tracks. The engineer wheeled round, almost stylishly. "Number One. What's up?"

"Tell me," Fowler began, closing the slight gap between them. "Do we have enough fuel to hold our position to get the helicopter back to Ascension?"

"Well …" said SH, putting his hands on his hips, sagely. "We were 95% full with fuel at Ascension, but we need the tanker White Rover to meet us up the nav-track for the last 800 miles from the Falklands and replenish from her. If that can't make it for any reason, we could run into stability problems and in seas like you get off the Falklands this time of year …" He tailed off realising the detail wasn't catching, and fixed Fowler's gaze. "Why?"

"Good," said Fowler, turning slowly away from him.

"Beg pardon?" SH was confused, and curious. Why was this 'good'? And why hold position? This bloke, who he barely knew, was really fucking strange.

"Oh!" chuckled Fowler. "Erm … good … er … answer. Thank you."

SH wasn't bought. Something was coming down the track and Fowler wasn't telling. "Why?" he pressed.

"Oh … er …I think we might need to get the Captain back to Ascension. I've just seen the doc. He says that it's some kind of virus … something he hasn't seen before." Fowler paused. "Thankfully, no-one else seems to have come down with the symptoms yet, but I suggested we get him off, before we all start dropping like ninepins."

"Is it that bad?" SH was genuinely concerned.

"I think so. Without the correct medical treatment, we could lose him."

"Shit!" gasped SH. "You sure? Do UK know?"

Fowler brushed this aside. "So, we might be flying both him and the doc to Ascension. We could get the RAF to transport the helicopter back down in a Hercules. That'll come later but I'll keep everybody posted. From now on, I'd better have conduct and control of the ship. We'll see what happens when we get to the Falklands."

"Yeah … let me know. I'll tell everyone else …"

"Good man," said Fowler and went forward, up a ladder and aft to the Captain's Cabin Flat. There, he stuck his head inside the curtained Captain's Pantry door, where Leading Steward Terry Fulwood, the Captain's own steward, was topping up a tumbler with Lemsip in it from a small, shiny electrical urn.

"Ah … Leading Steward Fulwood! How is he?" Fowler said.

Fulwood was an early thirties, discretely closeted, but effeminate gay man. Many on board lampooned his campness and speculated about his homosexuality, but no one really gave much of a fuck. Captain Belmont was exceptionally fond of him, and they'd had two or three private conversations about Fulwood's status where Belmont had pledged to support Fulwood in any way he could. But he made no real secret of his sexuality. Whenever there was a party, he was the one who would drag-up and was supremely hilarious with it. And he was as hard as nails for a 'brown-hatter' as the unsavoury naval moniker went. "Oh!" he said, rolling his eyes and clutching his fist to his chest. "Gave me a right start you did there, sir!"

Fowler didn't like gay people, at all. Fulwood continued, "he's not much better. Looks quite dreadful, in fact."

"Is that for him?" said Fowler, gritting his teeth through Fulwood's slight melodrama.

"Yes, it is sir."

"I'll take it in for him. God some good news." Fowler held up a buff-coloured, official file with 'CLASSIFIED' stamped across the top.

"Right you are, sir," said Fulwood, winking. "Coffee?"

Inwardly, Fowler's guts again wrenched a bit. "Yes please. I'll be about ten minutes …" and he disappeared through the next curtained door into the darkened Captain's day-room, lit only by the light on the desk. Underneath the light an ornate brass name plate, skilfully crafted by some naval artisan, bore the inscription:

Captain Stuart Belmont MBE

Royal Navy BSc (Hons) MA

He placed the glass on the Captain's desk and checked to see that he wouldn't be disturbed. He then fished a cellophane wrap from his pocket and tore the corner, emptying the contents into the yellow mixture and taking a gold pen from the desk-tidy stirred the drink. Fowler then slid the pen into his own top pocket, he then went through another curtain into the sleeping quarters.

Sunday, 27th September 1988
0640

Lynx HAS3GM XZ239 sat with rotor blades turning and punching the air percussively on the flightdeck in a grey, pitching ocean. Forward of the helicopter in the shelter of the hangar, Captain Stuart Belmont lay in a wheeled stretcher fully flight-suited with a white helmet on. His lips were dry, and he mouthed ineligible, delirious words lost in the cacophony of beating rotors and the aircraft's screaming Gem gas turbine engines. The Ship's doctor and his Petty Officer medical assistant knelt by the stretcher wating for a signal from the front door of the hangar. The medical assistant looked down and noticed the Captain was speaking and lowered his ear, clad in noise attenuating headphones, down to Belmont's face. Belmont couldn't raise his voice. Ten minutes ago, Fowler had helped him down three quarters of a glass of water, laced with generous amounts of benzodiazepine and methaqualone which he'd stockpiled at home courtesy of his now ex-wife. Belmont mouthed, "Something's wrong ..." but it was completely inaudible to the assistant. Taylor hadn't seen symptoms like these in his short career as a Medical Officer and needed Belmont off the ship and in someone else's hands before the it went out of range, and Fowler had detailed him to accompany Belmont and catch a flight down to the Falklands to rejoin the ship. The signal finally came from the WAFUs and the stretcher was wheeled up to the hangar door. Ten seconds later the Flight

This Fouled Anchor

Commander gave his own signal from the pilot's seat on the aircraft to bring the stretcher to the side door and load Belmont into the cabin behind him and the navigator. This was done effectively by the well-disciplined pair of WAFUs, one of whom was dressed in full flight gear. The medical assistant was called forward to assist and he shook the doc's hand before rolling the side door shut and returning to the hangar. The helicopter paused like some giant thundering hornet, it's anti-collision lights flashing scarlet and emitting a sense of awesome engineering peril. Without seemingly being prompted, the Flight Deck Officer received permission from the Bridge to launch 'two-three-nine' in his own headset and gave distinct signals to the Flight Commander who purposefully twisted his left hand to increase power whilst pulling the same hand slightly upwards. The aircraft increased its noise-level exponentially and began to lift from the moving ship, the Flight Commander steadying the craft using his right fist and feet. It rose to twenty feet above the deck, nodded leftwards and allowed *Warwick* to escape from beneath her. Suddenly she tilted and shot off down the port side of the ship.

Up on the Bridge, Fowler watched the action on the flight deck from the closed-circuit television monitor. He then watched the Lynx rocket off noisily past the port bridge window, climb, twinklingly into the grey sky, bank to starboard and head off on a direct line back to Ascension Island. A communique was received an hour ago from Northwood back in the UK giving him conduct of the ship and details of how the RAF were making plans to ship '239' down to the Falklands in the belly of a Hercules so the ship could be operational again. If all went well, the aircraft would likely beat them to the destination.

Fowler watched the helicopter into the distance until just a vague red twinkling could be seen just above the horizon.

"That was fucking easy," he said lowly to himself.

Chapter Eight

Sunday, 26th September 1988

1420

Daily routines on British warships generally reflect those back on dry land. However, once Fowler had rid himself of his pesky superior, he set the ship's staff to work in the 'Daily Routine' of a weekday with normal 'daywork' finishing at 1600. Today, even the day of the Christian Sabbath, was no different however come half-one, most of the crew had migrated to their messdecks in a disgruntled manner trying to pick up some rest and recreation.

Someone had broken out the Uckers board again in 3 November Stokers mess and a feisty game of doubles was underway. In the Red/Blue team, the top seed pairing of Ian Rees and Colin Parsons are resoundingly thrashing the hapless pairing Tanzy and Nige on Yellow/Green to the thumping sound of *'Somewhere In My Heart'* by Aztec Camera on the mess stereo. Ian's last throw rocked up behind Nige's 'four-piece-mixy-blob', itself blocked by Ian's own 'blob' in front of that and consigned the whole stack back to the start. It was classic hack-and-slash Uckers tactics, and now predictably Ian would 'timber-shift' his counters round the remainder of the board and catch Tanzy's, committing them humiliatingly back to the start with deft throws and some sleight-of-hand-cheating. A few others were being dragged into the excitement of it all, each cheering the winning team's concluding moves simply to piss Tanzy off, who loathed losing at Uckers and really, losing at anything. Ian's turn. He stood up.

"And now, assembled fiends, fishheads and knobheads … people of the world … I have a dream …" he said, grinning wide and picking up the dice.

Tanzy, sat at right angles to him with his overalls down by his ankles at Harry's insistence looked up, resigned and beaten. He knew what was coming. "If he fucking throws numbers again, permission to kick his fucking head in and get away with it, Harry?"

"Granted," said Harry, stood with a mug of tea. Someone had also opened the beer fridge as it was God's dedicated day of rest and Nige swigged a cool tin of McKewon's Red Label beer.

Ian rolled the two dice between his palms and blew on them. "Are you two fucking jizzmoppers ready? *Are you fucking ready?*" He threw. Six-six. It took two counters home.

"Cunt!" yelled Tanzy, and he meant it. Ian had another throw, which he did straight away. Another double six. The crowd wailed and cackled, and it took the remaining counters one step from 'home'. All he needed was 'snake-eyes', the double-one.

"I don't know why you and Nige do this to yourselves Tanzy," said Harry. "He's a numbers-throwing, timber-shifting bastard. I never play him. I'd rather fight Mike Tyson."

Ian took up the dice and people went silent. Ian tapped the dice on the table, paused for effect and tossed them. Double-one. By the time he had time to move his counters and win the game, Tanzy had flipped the board again in a move known as 'up table'. Counters, dice two tins of beer and an ashtray went airborne, and Tanzy followed straight across into Ian, dragging Colin with him. Again, there was a massive play fight between Stokers and Leading Stokers half dressed in overalls, all grunting and sweating with a hysterical Ian Rees on the bottom of the pile. Atky climbed onto the mess bar and launched himself airborne, fists-first, his sixteen stone of raw muscle impacting on the body pile bringing "oofs" and gasps from those under it. Harry stood up, dismayed the ashtray and some beer cans had been upset and Roy moved well clear from the melee. Somewhere under it, Tanzy's voice would be heard screaming as Colin had hold of his genitals and wasn't letting go, even when they spilled out of his pants.

"Fuck's sake!" yelled Harry once again. "Pack it in, you cunts. It's always this fucking way. Stop it!"

Just then the mess door swung open, and Fowler filled the frame. The fight continued but everyone in sequence looked up and saw the man looking back at them with a look of scorn and contempt. Nige, who'd stayed away from the struggle, froze with his beer almost at his mouth and Atky rolled off just leaving a man-lock of Colin, Tanzy and Ian. All suddenly realised something was up and released each other. Tanzy quickly tucked away his cock and balls in his ripped underpants.

"So, this is how you all choose to live your lives, is it?" said Fowler. "I do believe," he said, pointing at Nige, "…

MEM McDonnell, that you are seventeen years old. Am I right?"

Nige lowered the beer can and hung his head. "Yes, sir," he said, like a whipped puppy.

"So, that makes you below the legal age to drink alcohol, yes?"

Nige nodded. "Yes, sir." He placed the can down on the table beside his knees. There was an uneasy shuffling from almost everyone. Nige was gonna get it. And so was almost everyone else. Fowler had busted them.

"And it's …" he looked up at the mess clock which was characteristically battery-less, hand-less had no glass in it and had four o'clock Magic-Markered on it, and then at his watch, "… fourteen-thirty. During an official working day. And you are drinking alcohol, not yours either because you are not old enough to be issued with beer." Fowler looked round. "I take it your beer fridge is unlocked?"

Dodger looked at Harry who was motionless, almost wanting to blend in with the furniture, the fucking coward, so he intercepted the question himself. He knew where this was going as beer keys, of which they always had illegal duplicates, were always officially issued at 1630 and recovered at 2230. Them were the rules, always to be bent. Get caught out though, and you only had yourself to blame. And they couldn't blame Nige for having his own stock of beer, because that was illegal too. Dodger thought quickly, possibly too quickly.

"I gave it him, sir. It was his birthday yesterday. I had it stowed from my ration." The excuse sounded piss-weak but almost credible.

"Ah," said Fowler, turning to Dodger. "Leader Long. One of ... what ... five ... six Leading Hands here. All condoning a contravention of Naval Law. Article 1809 – "it is the duty of every Leading Rating of every branch of the service to ensure that order and regularity are preserved in his vicinity among those men, of whatever branch and whether duty or not, who hold a rating junior to him." Fowler was good, thought everyone, without exception.

Sullen, lowered looks came back, particularly from the killicks. Fowler continued, "Are you carrying out this ... Rees ... Barnes ... Atkinson? What about you, Leading Hand of the Mess, Leader Wilmot, isn't it?"

Harry replied, "Yes, sir," almost sounding tearful and upset about it all.

"And, of course, ever present in times of trouble is my dear friend, Leader Long. I can't expect you to follow the duties and responsibilities of a Leading Hand, *can I*?"

He brought his open hand down hard on the bar top with a thump, startling everyone being bollocked. The only sound was that of the ventilation. Ten people wanted to disappear into the pump space below the mess square but one was enjoying every moment of this.

"Okay. I want the beer fridge emptying now, the contents returned forthwith to the canteen and all funds submitted to the Master-At-Arms. Your beer privilege is stopped indefinitely." Fowler turned and jabbed, "McDonnell, you are in the shit, big-time."

He then turned back to the assembled rabble. "Think lucky, Leading Hands, that I don't exercise the full weight of Naval Law to punish you as well. I'm quite within scope to remove those Fouled Anchors from you all, but I can ill-afford the loss of six Leading Hands on my ship, for now. Stay well out of my line-of-fire. You are *all* noted. Now … all of you. Get the fuck back to work."

He then left into the lobby and slowly ascended the aluminium ladder outside. It wasn't until his steps upward had stopped and all knew he was out of earshot that anyone moved, let alone spoke.

"Sorry, guys," said Nige. Atky picked up Nige's beer can and handed it back to him.

"Happy birthday, shipmate," he said. "Fuck Fowler."

"Don't worry about it, son," said Harry, who'd stepped forward from the back and put his arm on Nige's shoulder. "The man's a fucking cock!"

"He's got to go," said Dodger, engaging Harry with a glare. "I've had enough of the bastard, already. Someone's got to do something."

"Such as?" Atky quizzed, pulling his overalls up and back on over his shoulders, ready to go back to work in the Chippie's Shop.

Throughout this, Jumper Crossley was behind the bar and had been reading a book until Fowler appeared. "Get the fucking hatches down!" he called, and sounded like he meant it, as usual.

Harry cut back across that line of thought like a buzz-saw. "Look, forget it, alright? I won't have any of that on my messdeck." He looked at Jumper, seriously. "Alright?"

"What?" said Tanzy.

"Dropping hatches. Mutinies don't work, and they never have. Remember the *Weymouth* when it went off on there in the Seamen's mess? Topsy Turner, you know, the killick of our Seamen's mess, he was in on it. He got fifty-six days over the wall. A right fucking palaver. Don't think there was anyone escaped scot-free – all eight or nine of them who just refused to work over an extra duty got banged up or booted out. They shut the hatches and paid the price. The system is just not built around that. We'd all be the losers." He paused. The assembled men hadn't bought it entirely and he knew it. "We'd just better shut the fuck up and get on with it. It's not for the likes of us to do that."

Everyone remained silent. Harry had just articulated the reality of being in a structured, disciplined armed service. Jumper didn't agree, however.

"Summat's got to be fucking done, Harry!" he said, prodding his finger into the bar top. "I can't stand six months of this fucker down the Falklands! I tell you, the more he gets away with, the worse he'll be. There's no-one to stop the fucking bastard now the fucking skipper's gone."

Chapter Nine

Thursday 29th September 1988

0915

Smith-Howlett and Lt Cdr Les Tremayne, *Warwick's* Weapons Engineer Officer sat in comfy armchairs in the relative plushness and order of the ship's wardroom. A few seats away reading the Times from 15 September sat Lt Cdr Tom Nicholson, the ship's Operations Officer. With the Captain embarked, all three constituted 60% of the 'Heads of Departments' or 'Hods', basically the executive of a warship. The only missing two were Fowler, currently luxuriating and masturbating in Captain Belmont's bath one deck above and the Supply Officer Lt Cdr Chris Braham, up in his cabin writing a letter home to his father, a decorated ex-Naval Admiral who now lived in Belgium.

"Y'know," said Tremayne. "My lads are in a real bad way. There's been a shitload of complaints from them. The Chiefs and Petty Officers are a bit snowed-under."

"I know Les. Thing is, he's bang to rights in most areas. What can we do about it?" SH was cool about the whole thing. It was what it was. Fuck that lot. This was his last trip.

"Well, I think it's just a matter of time, at this rate. We're heading that way I think," said Tremayne, lowering his voice a bit and making to look around.

"What 'way'?" said SH, scornfully.

"Well … you know …" Tremayne gestured with his head and his chin.

SH didn't get it. "No, Les … I don't …"

"Well … well … mutiny," he added, almost in a whisper.

Nicholson looked up and then quickly back down at his newspaper. It was quite clear he wasn't reading the article on Hurricane Gilbert smashing Jamaica up anymore.

SH made it public, though. "Aw, gimme a break, Les! You're out of your bloody tree. Who's been feeding you all this shit, eh? God in Heaven!" He sat forward, trying to bring some reason into the debate. "Sure, he's working the lads hard. Sure, they're pissed off. But it's all good team building stuff, yeah? We've got a long time away, with two hundred-odd men with little to do. We've got to keep them busy! My lads are suffering too. But at my stage of the career, I'd rather them be hating him, than hating me. I retire in under two years. I don't need the hassle. He's doing my job for me. As long as the screws turn and we go forward, who gives a shit? I've had a few ships in my time … "

Tremayne wasn't taken in by SHs apparent candour. "… yes, but this bloke is clearly off his rocker …" he said, his face darkening. This was serious shit.

SH paused and threw up a hand. "What do you want me to say?"

Nicholson got up, folded his paper and placed it on the chair, and left the wardroom. SH and Tremayne watched him go then the MEO fixed Tremayne with a stare, using his hand, flat and bladed to add emphasis to his point.

"There's no way that we, as senior Officers, can mandate any form of rebellion. All of us … and I mean, all of us, would be lynched. I know this, and I have seen it before. I'm too close to my pension to start rocking the boat, this boat in particular. Pat will take us down to the Falklands, we'll get another skipper before we set out on our first patrol, and he'll settle back in. By Christmas all this shit will be forgotten, and we can have a nice deployment and visits on the way back. I think he's a bit fearful that soon after joining he's suddenly driving the ship. That's all there is to it." SH sat back and pulled a cigar out of his shirt pocket and lit it. Squinting out the smoke, he added, "and if it ever came to the stuff, you're imagining us, and the Chiefs and Petty Officers would be dutybound … by military law … to back him up and retain order and conduct, come what may."

"He's got us all closed up at State 1 Action Stations tomorrow," said Tremayne, lowly. "What the fuck is that meant to achieve?"

"Well, at least it will bring the ship's company together as a team and prove our warfighting and internal battle systems work. We are heading into a zone of conflict, you know. The Argentines could kick off at any time and we will be the only warship down there now they've cut it down to one platform." SH's meagre attempt at justifying Fowler turfing everyone out of bed early to go to Action Stations all day wasn't working at all for Tremayne. To him it would further destroy morale and alienate the Officers from the Senior Ratings and then from the Junior Ratings. SH had an easy task in the Damage Control Headquarters directing firefighting and damage control teams to respond to simulated incidents, and Tremayne himself had the exercise sat by the side of

Fowler, now as Captain, in the darkened Operations Room advising him on weapons and sensors. He wasn't looking forward to that. Elsewhere though the rest of the 260 staff on the vessel were busy or bored, depending on where your position was.

Friday 30th September 1988
0650

"This is the Pee-Who from the Ops Room," announced the main broadcast, loudly and authoritatively. "Enemy forces detected in our sector, range three-zero miles. Argentine aircraft airborne and inbound. Intelligence suggests one Super Etendard armed with Exocet and two Daggers and three Skyhawk A4. Therefore ..."

The Main Broadcast Alarm sounded, it's bitonal stridency cutting through everyone now dressed in full Action Working Dress, fireproof number eight uniform with overalls on top and anti-flash hoods and gloves. It was uncomfortable, restrictive and hot. Everyone got moving without much conversation. Roy simply went up one deck to the Aft

Damage Control Section Base and plonked himself on the floor in exactly the same position he and Alex sat on the same class of warship six years ago. On his opposite watch he was stationed down in the noise and heat of the After Engine Room, stood between the Rolls Royce Tyne gas turbine ready to take control of them if remote control failed and give propulsive power back to the Bridge.

The PWO continued over the broadcast system, "Hands to Action Stations! Hands to Action Stations! Assume Damage Control State 1, Condition Zulu."

Harry Wilmott arrived, stood over Dodger with a Breathing Apparatus control board, rubbing out previous readings using his anti-flash glove. "Y'all right mate?" he said. Harry knew this wasn't easy for Dodger. He was also in the heat of the fight in 1982 but on another destroyer, badly damaged and taken out of the conflict by an air raid which fired an unexploded 1000lb bomb straight through one of its machinery spaces. Harry's ship limped home, but he recognised that characteristic on people like Dodger's faces who'd been through the wringer and out the other side when the fact dawns on you other human beings want you wiped the fuck out. Harry's cousin was also a Welsh Guardsman, missing presumed dead in the Argentine Airforce attack on *RFA Sir Galahad* at Bluff Cove on 8 June 1982.

Dodger held up a gloved thumb. "I love pointless fucking exercises, me," he said behind the meshed 'nosebag' which covered his face. "A day out of anti-flash is a day wasted in my opinion."

The Main Broadcast cut in again. "This is the Pee-Woh from the Ops Room. Enemy aircraft approaching at twenty miles, strength four. Air threat warning now, red!"

Dodger pulled his nosebag up, leant sideways against a portable pump and closed his eyes waiting for the first 'attack'.

1210

The Junior Ratings Dining Hall was almost full of men clad in overalls, many of them pulled down to their waists and tied off. Underneath, their Number 8 uniforms are saturated, either with the grime and sweat of fighting what naval strategists call 'the internal battle' or seawater from leaking firefighting hoses that Fowler insisted being 'charged' up to their closed nozzle ends. Everyone had their anti-flash hoods pulled back and were nursing bowls of scalding hot 'pot mess', which is an ad-hoc, but usually delicious stew made cheaply and quickly from any available ingredient to hand by the chefs for breaks in the action to get ship's crews quickly replenished. Made with care and with fresh, galley-baked bread it was like Manna from above and filled and nourished even the most desperate soul.

Dodger sat at one of the tables opposite Keith Osborne, the Leading Hand of the large Weapons Engineering messdeck further aft from 3 November. Keith was a decent chap in his mid-to-late thirties who, like Harry, had a sizable number of youngsters, idiots, problem children and weirdos to be daddy to in his mess. As he and Dodger ate, table manners took a break absent and they stuffed the stew down, greedily. Suddenly the main broadcast clicks in.

"D'you hear there! Captain speaking!" It is Fowler.

Dodger looked at Keith over a spoonful of lobby. "He's 'the Captain', now, is he?" said Keith. Dodger shrugged and raised his eyebrows. Now Fowler considered himself 'Captain'. That was a new one.

Fowler continued. "Today's damage control exercise was my first chance to see you all at action in the event of an attack. I am unimpressed to say the least. Although there were a few good areas, much of the exercise was carried out in a lacklustre and careless manner by you all, particularly the Junior Rates. It was evident that this ship is not prepared for a tour of duty on Southlant where we could be brought to bear on a potential threat at immediate notice."

Everyone, without exception, stopped eating. "To that end, there will be a repeat of proceedings at the same time tomorrow and be warned, I expect a massive improvement in attitude, or we will be doing it again, and again ... and again until we get it right. That is all." Fowler clicked off the microphone.

"Fucking wanker!" yelled a voice, further down the Dining Hall.

Fowler clicked the broadcast again. "The Ship's Welfare Committee Meeting will take place tomorrow in the Wardroom at fourteen hundred. All messdeck welfare representatives are to be mustered in the Wardroom at thirteen-fifty."

"What the flying fuck have we ended up with here? He's off his fucking box, mate," said Keith. "Cunt has totally fucking lost it."

"Is he ever," said Dodger, who carried on spooning stew in his mouth.

"We've got to clean up after lunch. Right state what with all that went on this morning. And we're doing it again tomorrow." Keith scraped the last morsels of pot mess out of his stainless-steel tray. He lowered his voice and leant forward toward Dodger. "You know, there's talk of 'down hatches' in our mess. Everyone is. Even the seamen, you know, Topsy Turner? He was on about it earlier."

Dodger raised his eyebrows again at this. Keith continued, "Oh, yeah. Topsy's done it before, on another ship, or summat. There's lots of talk about. Nob'dys got the guts though. Most of them down below are too fucked up to do anything. Shame about that. The more this wanker gets away with it, the more cack he'll drop on us. It's the law."

Dodger rises and picks up his tray and plastic mug, slinging his respirator and lifejacket over his shoulders. He leaned forward, his face close to Keith's and spoke lowly. "Shipmate, if you do intend to down hatches, count me in.

I've had a gutful of this fucker. Just an hour or so should do the trick. Hopefully the Wardroom and Senior Rates would talk him down and the prick will ease off."

Keith also rose. "I'll keep it in mind," he said. "Can't see it happening, though!"

2133

Dodger lay on his front in his bunk, writing a letter home to his mum which he hoped would be sent when they arrived in the Falklands. His bunk light lit the page, and his curtain was drawn across to give him privacy. He wrote:

> *Dear Mum*
>
> *It's been busy as hell over the past few weeks. We've been working like Trojans for the past fortnight, but the weather has been superb. I'm…*

He stopped, signed and yawned, rubbing his eyes with his non writing hand. Then he placed the pad under his pillow, switched off the light and settled down. They were all up early again tomorrow and he was up at 0345 to do the first part of the morning watch before Fowler took them into Action Stations again.

Saturday 1st October 1988

1150

Warwick finally fell out from Action Stations, once again. The previous six hours had been difficult with three simulated attacks on the ship and numerous raids and incidents for them all to deal with. Everyone was knackered, even the Officers and Senior Ratings. And as soon as the pot mess was served and over with, the Junior Rates set to work making the ship spick and span again, cleaning up the detritus and seawater, mopping and polishing flats in angry, impotent silence. No word from Fowler yet as to how they'd performed – if there was any improvement or even another episode tomorrow. Most took his silence as satisfaction or approval, but in truth he had more swords to drive into their collective body, like a strutting, preening toreador laying his cape low in the sand.

1435

The ship's Welfare Committee Meeting. Nine representatives of the ship's messdecks gathered on a monthly basis to thrash out problems and grievances, democratise decisions as much as possible and create an atmosphere of 'we are listening to you' across the three structures of Officers, Senior Ratings and Junior Ratings. Even if they are really not listening and just ticking boxes.

The Executive Officer always presided over this committee. Fowler was doing so, and he was under a line of gathering fire. But he is handling it masterfully, without compromise and utilising a level of Machiavellian mendacity way above the assembled rump of disgruntled largely Junior Rates. The last agenda item dealt with something close to sailor's hearts.

"... so, that's the rules, and for the foreseeable future, six of the Junior Rating's mess-decks will remain without their beer privileges. You lot broke the rules and until I can trust you not to fuck up again, it will stay that way. I mean what I say. Next item."

The secretary of the meeting, Leading Writer 'Chats' Harris stared for a moment at Fowler. His own mess was under stoppage. He broke out of his gaze and looked down at the agenda he'd carefully compiled. He biro-ed through the last item, knowing when he returned to his mess down aft later, the occupants were gonna blame him by association at their enforced teetotalism.

Able Seaman 'Bradders' Bradley, of the Seaman's mess suddenly stood up, foreshortening the procedure. He was bristling with indignation and rage at the last decision. "Sir," he said, slightly disrespectfully. Fowler loved this, pissing these little cunts off.

"Sir," continued Bradley. "I've been asked by the lads down our mess to ask why the ship's television system is switched off at half-past-ten every night. It used to be on all the time, and we could watch videos and stuff …"

Fowler looked purposefully, but with the right amount of authority at Bradley. "Able Seaman Bradley ... my good man," he began. "Pipe down is at ten-thirty at night. That means all lights off and you lot tucked up snugly in your little fart-chariots. No smoking, all beer fridges locked, keys returned, as per Standing Orders." Fowler smirked. "Those of you who have beer, that is. To me, AB Bradley, there is no other argument. Matter closed."

There were gasps of 'what?' and shaking of heads, around the table. The Chiefs and POs Mess representatives stayed silent but exchanged furtive glances. They were okay for now. Their privileged bar facilities complete with spirits and draught beer on a tab system remained intact. Fowler knew this and was using it as leverage for their loyalty.

"But ... sir ...?" Bradley continued.

"Able Seaman Bradley. Are you arguing with the Commanding Officer of this ship?"

"No, sir," Bradley backed immediately down.

"Good. Now sit the fuck down. Next?"

Jumper Crossley, the Stoker's Mess representative stood up, taking everyone by surprise. "Sir! I want to know why you are being so fucking smarmy about this?" he said, angrily pointing at the officer, spittle flying from his mouth. All heads and eyes locked onto Crossley, save for the Chief's Mess rep, who sat staring down in his lap. This wasn't going to be pleasant.

"It's not a committee, this. It's a fucking whitewash! Are you ever going to fucking listen to us? You don't give a toss! You sit there, all fucking smug, puttin' us all down! You don't give a fuckin' shite!"

Fowler sat motionless, not even moved by this outburst. "Crossley," he said. "Sit down." Crossley remained standing, checking himself slightly and relaxing the aggressive posture.

"SIT DOWN … I said!" Fowler banged the table, angrily. Crossley sat, slowly and purposefully, and folded his arms sullenly. A line had definitely been crossed here, and he knew it. Fowler snatched up the agenda in front of it and scrunched it, waving it around at the assembled men.

"I will tell you all this. Not one of you here has any such rights on board a British warship. My warship, by the way. So, you can forget your list full of bloody whinging, your weak protests at getting your beer back … your miserly whining at having to do extra work and keep this damned ship clean. You've all shown me what substandard sailors you are with the piss-poor performances during Action Stations yesterday and today. You can just get yourselves in shape for a tour of duty in which you will all … all … earn your daily wage as defenders of British territory." He paused and glared at everyone. All had fear and foreboding in their faces. What the flying fuck was this man on?

Fowler continued, now on a roll, "Gentlemen, there are going to be some radical changes around the ship … and I'm not sorry that it's going to affect you all."

He looked at the two senior ratings sat at the table. "I have the full backing of the Chiefs and Petty Officers in implementing these changes … so … my cheerless bunch of Welfare Committee representatives … take this good news to your constituencies …"

1455

Nearly every member of 3 November was packed into the mess square. Harry Wilmott had called a 'clear lower deck' of his charges when Jumper Crossley arrived back fifteen minutes ago and laid on him what Fowler had just laid on the

Welfare Committee. Crossley is finishing his piece to a haze of cigarette smoke.

"… so, he says that we are only allowed the one day per watch ashore wherever we go. Leave finishes at midnight, in every port we visit on the way back. He's even going to cancel the visit to Montevideo in Uruguay. Says we don't need to go."

This is met with gasps of 'no way!' and 'shit!' from the Stokers. The Uruguay visit, halfway through this trip over Christmas was eagerly anticipated. As was the proposed visits to Salvador de Bahia in Brazil and the Azores on the way home. Crossley continued, "And he wants us working until we hit the Falklands. No days off."

"What about the fucking beer?" said Ian Rees.

"What do you fucking think?" shrugged Crossley.

"What a cunt!" exclaimed Ian Rees. And he hardly swore like that.

Tanzy Lee stubbed out a cigarette into the top of an empty can of Fanta orangeade in front of him on the table. "This is going too far," he said. "He's on a wind-up. He's got to be kidding. If he's not …" he tailed off. "Summat's got to be done." There was equal parts desperation and determination in his voice.

Dodger leant up by the door with his arms folded and his eyes on Wilmott. The Leading Hand of the Mess leaned forward, staring down at the brown carpet. Suddenly he looked up and caught Dodger staring at him. "What?" he said, faking innocence.

"If you're not gonna do anything, then I fucking will," said Dodger, still looking purposefully at Wilmott. There was a rustle of anticipation from the assembled men.

"What you gonna do, Dodger?" chipped in Tanzy. Dodger said nothing, turned, opened the mess door and left.

Chapter Ten

2035

The end gulch in the Stoker's mess bunkspace was darkened. Three Leading Hands are sat on the bottom bunks, one of them being Dodger. The curtain at the end of the gulch opened and two more men entered. Dodger stood and allowed one of the men his 'seat'.

The men 'hutched across' to allow each other sufficient space to sit comfortably. They greeted each other with hushed tones – because other people are in bed elsewhere in the bunkspace – and because of the content of their potential discussion. Those present were the Leading Hands of most of the Junior Rating's messdecks on *Warwick*, with Harry Wilmott absent.

Those present were John Fisher from the small, twelve-man Stores Accountants' and Stewards' mess, 'Doc' Savage, a tubby Leading chef, dressed still in his galley whites, apron and hat of the Chefs mess, Keith Osbourne, and the ubiquitous and aggressive 'Topsy' Turner from the largest messdeck on the ship, the fifty-two-man Seamen's mess. Dodger starts the talking, in hushed tones. He felt way out of his depth doing this, and expected to be outflanked quickly, but was also surprised that so many had actually turned up. Only the Gunners mess up forward failed to send their killick, although Dodger had made the call through one of their mess's other Leading Hands. There was historic animosity between the Gunners and Topsy's Seaman's mess, for a vast multitude of largely childish reasons. Dodger knew this wasn't going to be easy, at all. He'd speak to the Gunners himself, later on, confident he could get them on board.

"First off lads, all I want to say is that something's got to be done about Fowler," he began, coming to a crouch to make his half-whispered voice heard above the background white noise of the ship's ventilation. Only Topsy looked engaged. He was grinning and nodding, almost insanely.

"Why?" said Fisher. "Where's Harry Wilmott?"

Dodger tried to put a lid on his exasperation. Fisher was an awkward fucker at the best of times, and he didn't like Stokers. He didn't like anyone outside his 'White Mafia' empire of the Supply and Secretariat branch in fact. "He's up in the Machinery Control Room, on watch." Dodger moved to rescue the point. "Listen … the whole ship is going to rat-shit. The fuckin' Senior Rates are completely fucked up about the whole scene … Fowler clearly fucking hates us … what we Junior Rates need is solidarity."

"Solidarity?" Fisher sneered. "Ha! What are you, Dodger? Some kind of lefty, union faggot? You fucking knob-end! Just fuck off, eh?"

"Dodge's right, Johnny-boy," interjected Keith Osborne.

"Why? What do you think you can do, eh? This whole fucking meeting's classed as a mutiny, now." Fisher made to get up. "I'm fucking going …" but Keith put his hand on his shoulder, to prevent him getting up.

"… hold on, Johnny. For fuck's sake, wait!" said Keith, and Fisher remained still. "Just … listen to Dodger, will you? We've got to make a stand. Fowler can't be allowed to get away with this shit any longer." Keith sounded genuine, and Fisher surprisingly, remained.

"Go on then, Dodger. Fuck him. I'm listening," said Topsy Turner. Dodger wasn't enamoured that the only positive feedback was coming from this head-the-ball. Quite how he'd become and remained a Leading Hand was often a conversation piece in many messdecks on *Warwick* especially after his previous 'incident' on his last ship. It took him three years to get his Leading Hand's badge back after that and he ended up on *Warwick*, strangely allowed to be Leading Hand of his Mess which at times was chaotic and disordered. Many of the other killicks down there despised him, but they were shit-scared of him. He was like a grenade with the pin already out most of the time.

"There's more of us than them," Dodger offered. "We've just got to drop the hatches on all the Junior Ratings messdecks for an hour or so, as a team. All of us. The ship would grind to a halt."

"A mass mutiny?" mused Doc Savage. He looked like Danny DeVito's elder, dirtier but slightly taller brother.

Dodger turned to Doc, as a way in. "It's simple! What are they going to do? Discipline all of us? Two hundred Junior Rates?"

Fisher still wasn't bought. "Oh, I don't know. If he's bad now, just think what he'll be like after a mass hatch-down. We'd be well fucked!"

"No. Just think," Dodger responded, this time directly to Fisher. "Word would get out easily. The top brass would replace Fowler. We'd get a new Skipper and another new Jimmy. Us lot would just get our wrists slapped. All you lot must do, as Killicks of messes, is ensure we get maximum support ... everyone involved. We just stay in touch ... and come out when we feel like it."

"Or we fucking starve, more like," added Doc Savage.

"Start stocking up then! You're the fucking chefs, aren't you? You've got all the keys to the storerooms and all that shit. Get everyone to start buying nutty from the NAAFI. It's only gonna be for a few hours, anyway. If we get enough, we could go on for days, if we want."

Faces were still unemotive and unconvinced.

"What about having a piss? Or a shite?" asked Keith.

"Bucket and chuck it," Topsy answered quickly.

"My mess and Doc's are upstairs on 2 deck," said Fisher, and Doc nodded in agreement. You lot are on 3 deck, with steel hatches between you and them. We've only got aluminium doors that will go in with a good kick. If they decide to move in on us from the passageways, we are out of it. We'll be the first to go."

Keith had a solution. "... in that case, my mess is below both of yours. We will leave our escape hatches open. If they do bust in and get heavy, just drop down to us. Then we'll button the escape hatches back up from below. They can't get at us then." No one added to this. It seemed sorted. Two or three conversations broke out between those gathered. It sounded like a plan was being formed. Dodger tried to get control back. "Lads ... lads ... quiet, eh? Look. We need to get this about, but to the right people. And we need to down hatches tomorrow, if possible, so that people don't get cold feet, or the word gets to the Chiefs and Petty Officers because those cunts won't back us up. They're all on Fowler's side. We're only three-and-a-bit days from the Falklands. One day will be enough, but if he decides to stretch it out, then fine. We've got to refuel from the tanker on Tuesday ... and they definitely need us for that. We can force a decision from him ..."

"Yeah ... what about the Chiefs and POs?" enquired Doc. He had a point. "The Senior Ratings would never back a mutiny. We'll probably have to deal with them too."

"Fuck 'em," added Topsy. "Fuck' em! I hate them all, anyway. If they get to know, they'd grass us up and we'd be in shit street."

"Yeah, you're probably right. By the sound of it, there's not many Chiefs and POs who would back us." Dodger wanted someone to add a comment. No one did. All eyes were on him. "We'd better keep this schtum … it's the surprise that will fuck Fowler up. Tomorrow, then?"

There was a pause. It was heavy with excitement, dread, foreboding, resolve, trepidation and fear. Keith broke it.

"Yeah! No time like the right time!"

Topsy stood up and puffed out his chest. "Let's fucking get it done! I'll tell the lads in my mess. They'll be up for this."

Everyone nodded and got up, bar Fisher, who was slowly shaking his head, clearly not bought fully on this lunacy.

"Tomorrow it is, then. I say we down hatches at, what … half-pest twelve," said Dodger, looking round at his co-conspirators. "That gives us ample time to grab lunch, and get enough food and drink in. Is everyone in on this, then?"

No-one responded negatively. Not even Fisher this time.

Sunday 2nd October 1988
1222

The mess lobby was a hive of activity. Boots thundering up and down the ladder and several Royal Navy Stokers dressed in their Number 8 working rig or overalls ferrying items back and forth in a relatively impressive display of teamwork. Some carried armsful of bread, cooked last night in Doc's galley, some bags of crisps and boxes of sweets. Others had rope and tools. Ian Rees picked up a length of the stuff from the bar top and threw it across to Jumper Crossley, stood with his brain in neutral for a moment, and not swearing or berating someone.

"Jumper. Go rope those escape hatches up in the bunkspace. Chop, chop ..."

The rope bounced off Jumper's shoulders and onto the deck. "Fuck you," he responded and left the compartment. Tanzy sighed and picked up the rope from the carpet and went out into the bunkspace.

Harry Wilmott appeared and crossed the mess square to Dodger, who is busily filling the beer fridge with victuals. "Dodger ..." he said, his voice wobbly with fear. "Dodger, you know … I don't like this shit. Let it be said that I said that. I was talking to Jon Fisher this morning and he said …"

"Aw, shut the fuck up, Harry," said Steve Hepplewhite. Dodger ignored the Leading Hand of the Mess in a move to blank out any misgivings he himself held, which in fact were multiplying. Harry was right. This was fucking madness. But so was allowing Fowler to continue his shit. He stood up and called across the bar. "Nige. Ring the other messes. Check they are all ready."

Harry persisted. "… look, Dodger! Do we have to go through with this? I mean … we'll all go in the shit … you … me … all the lads. It'll be murder!"

Dodger rounded on him, with a look of resolve. "Harry, it's got to be done. In …" he pointed up at the clock, still not working with the magic marker on it, "… six minutes, the hatches go down and Fowler will see his career disappear. You've got to be cruel to be kind. Do you want to live like this for six fucking months? With that prick? Well, neither do I. So, fucking-well start pulling in the same direction, eh? The lads are so up on this idea, they'd probably murder you if you stood in their way." Wilmott's face dropped.

Nige McDonnell replaced the handset on the mess phone, announcing triumphantly, "Dodger? Everyone's ready. Galley's empty, dining halls ... the fucking lot!"

"Nobody's pulled out?" asked Dodger. Nige shook his head.

"Our lads down from the Machinery Control Room?"

Mick Parsons bustled past, carrying a beige paper gash bag. "Yep. I'm last man."

Dodger fixed a look on Harry Wilmott. "Tanz ... do the honours, will you? Lash it tight."

Tanzy had just returned from his last job and picked up another roll of rope. "On me way love ..." he said. Both he and Nige went out into the lobby where the ladder connected the mess upwards with the 2 deck. Tanzy rose a few steps up the ladder and unclipped the heavy steel hatch from its wall lock. He gently started down the ladder, controlling the weight on its way down. Halfway down, a Chief Petty Officer passed, taking a cursory glance at Tanzy who offered, "'Afternoon, Chief!" and lowered it all the way down resting it on its raised sealing coaming. Both Stokers then latched on the retaining clips, quickly and started to secure them with the rope. A small crowd of spectators started to gather from the mess-deck in the lobby. They were all looking up at Tanzy, silenced by the monumental significance of this action, taking place before their eyes.

Tanzy finished lashing the hatch clips secure and turned. "Done!" he said, brushing his hands.

Everyone filed back into the mess square area, and sat down on the covers, still silent. Mick Barnes sat next to Dodger, pulling out packet of Benson & Hedges from his top overall pocket and offering one habitually to Dodger. Dodger took the cigarette and lit it from Mick's lighter, sitting back luxuriously, staring at the ceiling and blew out a long column of smoke. That felt good. Real good.

Chapter Eleven

1250

Fowler sat at the desk in the Captain's Cabin with the Operations Officer Lt Cdr Tom Nicholson positioned nervously on the bench sofa across from him.

"So, how has the ship's company taken to the new routine, then?" he prodded at Nicholson, who in turn twitched and ticked at being addressed in such an aggressive manner. Nicholson was good at his job as Ops Officer, but his underlings found him weak and prevaricating. His ambition was Command of a proper warship like *Warwick* one day instead of the patrol vessel *Lundy* which he was driving fifteen months ago. People like Fowler scared the shit out of him though and he lacked the potatoes to stand up and be 'the man' much of the time, relying on people in his team to do the real decision making whilst he surfed on their collective leadership. In short, he was pretty crap as a Lieutenant Commander and easily bullied. "Well, as far as I know, things are okay ... a few drips here and there ... but, hah! Sailors, eh? Hah!" he added, shrugging and trying to humour Fowler. Fowler's eyes darkened.

"What's the matter with my ship's company, eh? Anyone would think they would prefer to be unemployed." He stroked his whiskery chin and then pointed at Nicholson. "They should show gratitude to me that I give them work." Fowler then sat forward, lowering his voice in a conspiratorial manner. "They're all bastards, you know. Fucking Junior Ratings. I'll show them."

Nicholson shifted uneasily in his seat, "What?"

"If they don't like it the way it is, then we'll move the working day from six in the morning to six at night. They don't know when they've had it so good!"

The telephone on the desk beep-beeped. Fowler snatched it up. "Captain?"

Petty Officer Crawford was on the other end. He was an impressive, all-arms trained gunner who'd spent some time on Arctic operations with 42 Commando Royal Marines and hence wore their green beret, albeit without the sought after and coveted Globe and Laurel badge. At six three, he was a bit of a slab and put himself about at times. "Sir," he said, standing opposite the firmly shut hatch of the Weapons Engineers on 2 deck. "We seem to have a bit of a problem."

"What is it, Crawford?" said Fowler, impatiently.

"Well, it looks like it's a mutiny, sir," came the reply.

"Mutiny?" Fowler spluttered. Nicholson flinched and jumped.

"Yes, sir. All the hatches to the Junior Rates' messes are down. Stokers, Greenies, S and S and the Seamen."

"Where are you now?"

"I'm, um … outside the Greenies mess on 2 deck, Quebec section. Me, the Chief Stoker, a couple of PO's … oh, and the Chief Ops has just arrived."

"Right," Fowler said. "I'll be right with you. Stay there!" He rose and clicked his fingers on one hand and said, "with me" to Nicholson, as though he was a lapdog. They exited the Captain's Cabin and through passageways, down ladders and onto 2 deck, the main thoroughfare of a Type 42 Destroyer which ran circuitously around the ship with two spur passageways at either end. It was on the after one of these that he found the gathering of Officers and Senior Ratings and of course, PO Crawford.

"All the Junior Rates' messes?" he said to the Petty Officer.

"All of them, sir," Crawford replied.

On either side of the passageway two firmly closed, polished aluminium doors led to the smaller twelve-man messes of the Chefs, Stores Accountants and Stewards. Fowler pointed at the starboard one, which had:

2 Quebec (Starboard)

Chef's Messdeck

By Appointment to HM Queen

proudly engraved on a brass plate in the centre of the door, tribute to Leading Chef Doc Savage's prior draft to Her Majesty's Royal Yacht *Britannia* and his role as one of her own personal chefs. Most of Savage's tales of this were long winded, tall, exaggerated and frankly full of shit. Right now, Her Majesty's Leading Chef stood on the other side of the door, holding the handle up as the lock was broken. Fowler crossed the passageway and tried the handle. It was solid but obviously being held upwards. He stepped back from the door, paused and then in a fit of pure rage, aimed a huge kick into the lower panel. It banged loudly and stopped any conversation in the passageway. Doc, on the other side called out, "You can huff … and you can puff …" to which his messmates, spectating in the dark cackled loudly. Fowler followed this up with six or seven hefty kicks to the door.

"Oooh! I say!" said Doc, camply.

Fowler turned to the gathering crowd behind him. Officer and Senior Ratings alike, he addressed them in the same angry, disrespectful manner. "You lot. Wardroom, right now."

Ten minutes later he stood at the head of the Wardroom dining table. Before him the remainder of the 'lower deck' had been cleared and all the Officers, Chief Petty Officers and Petty Officers were present, nervously shuffling and avoiding each other's gazes. Some of the younger Petty Officers were mumbling to each other near the back until Fowler cut them silent.

"Is that everybody? Yes? Okay. Listen in. *Quiet!* Listen in, now. Right, Gentlemen. Because of a severe collapse in management and therefore, a hitherto slump in discipline, to which I hold you all responsible, we have what amounts to a mutiny on our hands. I will say this now … if I find that any of you are aligned in any way, shape or form to this uprising, I will press for the maximum punishment." He looked at everyone angrily. "Do I make myself perfectly clear?"

A muted, "Yes, sir," came back at him.

"Now then," he continued, angrily glaring at those present. "We are going to deal with this quickly, effectively, and incisively. We will not stop the ship, nor slow its advance. *HMS Athene*, is awaiting our arrival in the Falklands so she can go home to the UK. We will press on with our programme and fulfil that commitment. Each of the Officers here will be assigned a number of Chiefs and PO's and utilising these men, we will systematically retake this ship, messdeck by messdeck and restore order. We will start with the easy targets, namely the 2 deck messes, the Chefs, first."

Lt Cdr Les Tremayne raised his hand. Fowler fixed him with a maddening glare. "Yes? WEO?"

"Don't you think we'd better talk to these people first, before making any rash overtures towards violence?" Tremayne's comments were met with stony silence. "I mean, we could find out what the problem is, come to some sort of compromise and ..."

Fowler exploded. "... COMPROMISE? You are suggesting that I negotiate with these ... these ... fucking crooks? I will negotiate, WEO. But my negotiation will be at their Courts Martial, when I see justice be done!" Fowler paused. He could see the terror and confusion in people's faces. "Right! I think I have made myself clear on the way ahead. Once one mess-deck falls, so will the others ... just like dominoes. MEO?"

Smith-Howlett chimed up, somewhere over near the bar area. "Yes?"

"I want all services to the Junior Rates messdecks isolated. Ventilation, power, heating, lighting and water. All off. I want you to get the Chief Shipwright to report to me his availability to cut through bulkheads and hatches with oxy-acetylene, if needed."

SH was stunned, especially at the prospect of gas-axing his precious warship up. "XO, is that necessary? I mean ..." he said but Fowler chopped him up.

"I don't want a fucking debate, MEO. Just get it done, right?"

"Consider it done," said SH, after a pause.

Fowler scanned those present, in a challenging manner. "Any more questions?"

There were none to be broadcast, but internally most thought, "what the flying fuck is going on?"

Outside 2 Quebec Starboard Chefs messdeck and in the adjacent passageways there were about thirty-five Officers and Chiefs and Petty Officers, either actively involved in Fowler's plan or jostling for a view. Behind the door, another chef held the handle, still dressed in his own galley whites, apron and white chef's hat. Nearest the door stood one Chief Petty Officer and five Petty Officers, dressed in overalls and combat boots, each carrying a small polycarbonate shield, a nightstick and all wearing dark blue helmets with the visors pulled down. In between them similarly dressed but in white overalls and not carrying a shield or stick stood the frankly petrified form of Lt Cdr Nicholson, the Operations Officer. Fowler approached him and motioned him down the passageway as if to brief him further or give him a pep talk. Fowler pulled Nicholson in and facing away from the rest of the raiding party and shoved a Browning 9mm automatic pistol in Nicholson's sweaty palm. "If in any doubt, fucking use it to restore order. I will cover for you if you do," he said, lowly. Nicholson looked down at the gun like it had just splattered out of the arse end of a bull onto his shirt. He was horrified. Fowler snatched it back and chambered a round, pushing it back in Nicholson's weak grip. Fowler then led the Ops Officer back to the group and called out, "Clear the area!" shoving spectators forward toward a cross passageway. Once there, he turned and gestured to Nicholson to proceed.

In the Chefs mess, Doc Savage was on the phone to Dodger.

"… yeah, mate. The lads in the mess opposite have got their hatch down to the Keith's mess open too." He looked over at the circular hole in the floor with the lights of the Weapons Engineers' messdeck shining through and activity below. Suddenly the lights went out and the ventilation noise stopped. Battery powered automatic emergency lights lit up the small mess square in an eerie glow. Doc's messmates looked upward at the extinguished light shades and then looked fearful.

"Whoa, Dodger! They killed the lights," said Doc.

"And the vent!" said another chef.

"You guys okay?" asked Dodger.

"Yeah, we'll survive, pal. They're right outside, now. There's a lot of movement in the passageway. How's the rest of the messes?" Doc lowered his voice a bit. He could now hear someone shouting through the door.

"Well buddy ... the Seamen are well battened down – Topsy's got them in good order. The Radio Operators have had their phone off the hook for the past twenty minutes. Hope they're okay. Last I spoke to them, they were missing one. Toby Faulkner. He's on the outside. Bet he's shitting himself."

"Poor twat," said Doc. "Dodge. How much food have you got?"

"Enough, I suppose. What about you guys?"

Doc chuckled. "Mate. We are the Chefs!"

Suddenly the mees door gave out two gigantic bangs. Doc shouted down the phone at Dodger, "Showtime, mate ..." and hung up. The chef holding the handle reeled back and the door came in and off its hinges with the third, sending the occupants scattering back into the darkened mess square. Two Petty Officers scrambled through with a roar and the chefs fearfully retreated through the narrow space between the kit lockers and bunks. More tooled-up Senior Ratings followed, and the front two chefs charged forward to stop the advance. Poly-shields went up in the air and night sticks were brandished but there was no room to swing them. A struggling, grunting fight broke out in the dim light with five or six men eventually tumbling to the tiled deck grappling and swearing. A helmet was ripped off one of the Petty Officers and swung and it contacted the second row of shields, more men clambering over the body pile and a hairy fist broke through, sparking one of the POs clean out, making him collapse sideways. In the mess square Doc screamed, "C'mon lads!" and started ushering his messmates down to the mess below through the escape hatch whilst the fight went on just yards away. Six people literally fell through the small hole trying to escape downwards with those below trying to catch them. The fight made it to the locked-up stage with three Petty Officers and two chefs brutally trying to exert leverage, punches, stick hits, anything on each other. Over the back of this appeared Nicholson with the nine-millimetre pointed straight out like and extension of his arm. Doc stood up, looked down at the people in the mess below through the escape hatch and kicked the circular cover into place so they could secure it from below. He then took out his boning knife from the leather scabbard in his apron, the same knife presented to him by Her Majesty the Queen on the *Britannia* - so the story goes - and held it out in front of him.

"C'mooooon, then, you fucking … fuckers!" he yelled, pulling off his galley cap. "C'MOOOONNNN!"

Nicholson settled the foresight of the pistol on the shape of Doc's head in the dim light. He instinctively squeezed the trigger and put a fat slug through it with a sharp bang, dropping the Leading Chef vertically as though every bone had been instantly removed from his body. Nicholson then fired a volley of three shots into the slumped form.

The cracks from the gunshots instantly stopped the fight, Nicholson still like a statue, gun held out, the sour smell of cordite in everyone's nostrils. The two struggling chefs submitted, and the three POs put them on their faces, one of them bleeding profusely from his nose and mouth. Crawford stepped forward and took the pistol off Nicholson, who now had tears streaming down his cheeks and was openly sobbing. The Chief Ops came in the mess and led him away, back forward and up to his cabin. Doc Savage lay dead, blood oozing from a vast hole in the back of his head all over the mess square floor, with the melamine bulkhead behind him spattered with brains, bone parts and what looked in the dim light like black engine oil.

Down below, everyone heard the gunshots and Doc Savage drop to the deck. This brought gasps of "fuck!" and "no!" from everyone looking upwards. One of the Weapons Engineers stood half on a bunk and wrestled with the strongback lever mechanism that secured the escape hatch in place, almost reversing the intended action of the equipment. As he wound on the screw, blood seeped through, dripping on his bare arm. It was still warm. He looked at it and then at everyone else.

"Fucking no way!" shouted Keith Osbourne, the Leading Hand of the large mess, real revulsion and anger in his Mancunian voice.

Back up in the Captain's Cabin, Fowler picked up the phone. Crawford was on the other end.

"Sir ... PO Crawford here," his voice unruffled.

"Yes?" said Fowler, expecting a resolution.

"'Sir, 'fraid to say ... Leading Chef Savage has been shot ... fatally ... by the Ops Officer."

"What about the mutiny?" said Fowler. "Is it over?"

"No sir. Some chefs escaped below into the WEs mess. We've taken two of them and they are in sickbay getting sorted. But Leading Chef Sav …"

"Yes … yes … I heard you Crawford." Fowler paused. "Fatally, you say?"

"Yes, sir," responded Crawford. Even he sounded somewhat regretful. "The POMA is now examining his body. He went for the raiding party with a knife."

Fowler couldn't give a fuck. "Right. Carry on. Next messdeck," he said. The Stewards and Stores Accountants in the fourteen-man mess opposite the chefs had already emptied downward through their own escape hatch once the lights went out and the shooting started. Apart from an already empty mess up on two-deck forward whose residents were safely in with the Seamen's mess, the next target to raid was one deck down, through steel, clipped hatches firmly roped shut.

In 3 November Stokers messdeck, the phone beeped and Dodger snatched it up. Before he'd got the chance to speak, Keith Osbourn's panicked voice blurted out of the earpiece.

"Dodger!" he screamed. "Dodger, they've fucking shot Doc Savage!"

Dodger checked himself. This was impossible information. "What?" he said. "How?"

"No shit, mate! They stormed the chef's mess about five minutes ago. The rest of them are all down here with us ...'xcept Doc. And a couple of others, I think." Keith then spoke with someone else with his hand over the mouthpiece.

"Keith ... who did? What ...?" Other's present near Dodger started looking at him fearfully.

Keith came back, "The Chiefs and PO's. Apparently, the Ops Officer was with them, and he was armed."

"Armed? Armed with what?" Everyone in the mess square then looked up, further alarmed when Dodger said this.

"Think he had a nine-mil. There's blood seeping down through the escape hatch, mate. If he was shot at that range, he's gotta be fucking dead."

Dodger felt giddy and slunk forward a bit. His gesture gave away to the rest of the mess what was building.

"What's happened?" said Steve Hepplethwaite. "Who ... who have they shot?"

"What's up, Dodger," said Tanzy, getting up off the carpet where he'd been playing Solitaire. He sounded like a little boy. Dodger waved him away.

"So, what now? Do the rest of the messes know?" he said.

Keith suddenly sounded centred and resolute. "I say we stay. Bastards are going to pay for this. Hang on … the lads from the Stewards and Caterers mess are down here, now. They've just stormed their gaff, as well."

"Anyone hurt?" asked Dodger.

"Not that I can see. Think they started to come down after the shooting began in Doc's messdeck …" Keith again started to speak to someone with his hand over the mouthpiece. Dodger became very pissed off, both with the impotency of the situation and with dealing with the fact that he could be responsible in some way for Doc Savage's death.

"Keith, sit tight. They can't get at you where you are. I'll ring the other messes to let them know the state of play. This is a fucking nightmare."

Chapter Twelve

1515

The lobby above 3 November Stokers mess is a three-way intersection between the two passageways leading up the port and starboard side of the ship and a single spur passageway leading aft to the quarterdeck. To the starboard side sat a steel hatch in the closed position, firmly held there by Tanzy's and Nige's ropework. The clips were hammered on tight from below and further held in place by a variety of means, making access from above impossible. The Stokers, like many other of *Warwick's* Junior Ratings, were sealed in and not coming out. Elsewhere in the ship the watchkeeping and roundsman tasks on the Bridge, Operations and Machinery Control Room usually carried out by the Junior Rate mutineers were now being begrudgingly covered by Petty Officers meaning a lot of hasty relearning of skills. Things were just getting by.

Fowler stood with SH and Tremayne and a few Chief and Petty Officers above the Stokers mess hatch. "Right," he said. "It's time we showed these little bastards we mean business. PO Crawford?"

Crawford stepped forward dutifully. "Sir?"

Tremayne interjected. "Um, Pat ... what exactly are you planning, here?"

Crawford respectfully but firmly eased past him. "CS Gas sir. Watch your back if I were you." He took two large, pill-like capsules out of a foil wrapper and brandished his *'HMS Warwick Gulf Deployment 1987'* Zippo lighter. Tremayne was a tad alarmed at this.

"Look ... c'mon, for Christ's sake!" he said, looking at Fowler and Crawford, each in turn. "You can't gas them out! You just morally can't do this ..."

"Can and will, WEO. Can and will." Fowler was unsmiling and serious. "As a youth, I used to go with my uncle Teddy and gas the fucking badgers out of their sets on his farm on the Isle of Wight. Easy, fucking-peasy."

Tremayne threw his hands up in the air and let out an exasperated gasp of "Bollocks!" Then he drew closer to Fowler, locking his stare. "Pat ... before you do this, I implore you ... please ... to let me speak to them on the phone. Just once. It may save a lot of grief. Please?"

Fowler returned his stare, almost seemingly enjoying the torment he was leveraging in on Tramayne's conscientiousness. Ten seconds passed before he said anything. Everyone froze.

"Okay," he said. "Don't take any fucking shit from them. If you don't get what I want, these go in." He pointed at the metal tray where the tablets sat in Crawford's hand. Tremayne walked over to the telephone, just inside the door of the After Switchboard Room, adjacent to the passageway. Still looking at Fowler, he dialled 3 November mess's number, two-five-five.

Just below where he stood, the mess square was in semi-darkness. People slept on the carpet wrapped in their overalls, some with sleeping bags over them. Tanzy sat up, reading a Commando comic by torchlight. Above his head, the phone beeped loudly, waking some of the Stokers. Tanzy reached up and took the receiver off the hook.

"Good afternoon," he said, still looking at his comic. "Good afternoon. Sea of Tranquillity, Captain Neil Armstrong, speaking." Tanzy was full of insolent charm such as this. SH had once rung the Machinery Control Room up and after a short conversation with him asked what Tanzy was doing. Convinced it was Mick Barnes putting on an accent he said, "Having a fucking wank with me thumb up me arse!" and hung up. This cost him five days stoppage of leave and a sixty-pound fine at the Captain's Table with Cdr Belmont struggling to suppress his mirth when the dialogue was read out.

"Ah! Erm … who is this?" It was clear this wasn't someone in one of the other Junior Ratings messdecks.

Tanzy sat up and bristled. "Tanzy. Tanzy Lee. Who's this? Is it you, Fowler, you fucker?"

Tremayne hoped Fowler couldn't hear Tanzy's response. "Er, no. Could I, erm, speak to Leader Wilmot, please?"

Tanzy was indignant. "Nope, 'fraid not. He's got his head down. Can I help you? Is this Fowler?"

"Are there any Leading Hands there?" asked Tremayne, still trying to be passive, but authoritative in equal measures.

"Certainly, standby …" Tanzy brusquely retorted and held the phone out to Dodger, who had woken and was shuffling across on all fours. "It's one of them cunts. He wants a grown-up, Dodger …"

Dodger took the phone. He'd only just dropped into a decent sleep and could feel the weariness in his eyes, "…yeah? Dodger Long here. Whaddya want?"

Tremayne tried the soothsayer stuff. "Look. Leader Long. This can't go on any longer, you know. It is utter madness."

Dodger wasn't having any of that nonsense. "You bastards shot Doc Savage," he said.

"Yes," said Tremayne. "It was an accident, Dodger. It couldn't be helped. We are currently sorting that out … look …"

Dodger was now fully awake. "That's a load of bullshit … and you fucking know it! What are you doing carrying guns for, anyway? None of us are armed! It's Fowler, isn't it? I tell you … he's fucking tapped in the head, he is …"

Tremayne decided that Fowler's last words about taking any shit from them was possibly the best way forward. He needed to be firm. "…Dodger, now listen. Come on, calm down now. Man to man. Either come out … or you and many others will live to regret your actions. You'll be gravely sorry for this. We mean it." Fowler glared at him and nodded. Tremayne continued, "I'm ordering you to open the hatches, and we can talk about this and sort this out. You must understand that there can be no concessions until you open the hatch and talk to us. The First Lieutenant …"

"Look, sir. I know there are some good officers in the Wardroom … possibly yourself included … but the bottom line is that we are out when Fowler steps down and someone else takes over. And we mean that." Dodger hung up abruptly. Tremayne looked up at Fowler and shrugged his shoulders. Fowler turned immediately to Crawford who clicked open his Zippo lighter and lit the CS pellets in the tray in front of him. With them sputtering and fizzing, he walked over to the closed hatch, unscrewed the large indicator test plug in the centre of the hatch and dropped the pellets in through the two-inch diameter hole. He lit two more and dropped them in. The passageway immediately started to fill with a small but significant amount of sour, stinging tear gas making all watching either cover their mouths and noses or splutter. Crawford replaced the test plug and looked up at Fowler, who had a blank, bleak expression on his face.

Just below the hatch in the mess lobby, all four pellets bounced off the ladder steps and landed on the deck, propelled in circles by the gas they emitted. The noxious cloud started to billow and form quite quickly.

In the mess square. Dodger sat with Tanzy and Harry Wilmott in the silent gloom. Many others are still fast asleep.

"... fuck 'em," said Dodger, defiantly. "I don't care. They shot Doc. We could be next, you know ..."

Suddenly Mick Barnes who was slumbering on a mess square seat near them sat bolt upright. "Dodger!" he said. "I can smell ... CS Gas!"

Tanzy responded. "Fuck! Yeah!"

Dodger jumped up. "Tanz, shake the lads, quick. Get everyone to get their rezzies on! QUICK!"

Tanzy exited the mess square, followed by most others. Everyone kept their Anti Gas Respirators in their boot lockers, in the bunk space next door. Colin Parsons had thundered out of his top pit, landed on someone below and stumbled out of the bunk space into the lobby, which by now was thick with tear gas. Suddenly so was the bunkspace, where more people were mobilising, trying to find their own bootlockers and respirators through the searing agony invading their eyes, noses, mouths and lungs. Suddenly a fight broke out in one of the gulches between Nige O'Donnell and Jumper Crossley. Both hung onto a single respirator bag and were hauling frantically, raining punches and they spluttered and coughed. Dodger and Harry Wilmott arrived having found and donned their own gas masks, and Jumper, being the stronger and heavier in the fight, managed to decouple Nige from his gas mask and push him on his arse. Very quickly, the respirator was out of the bag and on Jumper's head. Nige laid crying, wheezing and coughing. "Dodger!" he spluttered. "Jumper's got my fucking rezzie!" Nige was truly struggling to breathe, saliva streaming out of his mouth and ribbons of snot from his nose. "Help me, please!" he sobbed, rolling over onto his front. Dodger turned toward Jumper, who backed off guiltily into a darkened gulch. Harry followed him.

"Jumper! For fuck's sake! Give the thing back to Nige! Now!" Jumper backed further into the gulch toward his own bunk. He slid one hand beneath his pillow, still looking at Dodger and Harry through his respirator lenses.

Harry stepped closer and Jumper whipped out a large hunting knife. Harry stopped. Everyone froze at the appearance of a weapon. Harry moved forward again.

"Jumper … hand over the knife … and give Nige back his rezzie. Now! Do as you're fucking told!" He stepped forward again, putting out his hand. Jumper lunged forward, stabbing

Harry straight in the chest. He pitched backward off the blade in reaction with a gasp, and a large plume of blood jetted out in an arc onto the floor. Harry fell backward, grunting to the deck and Dodger tried vainly to catch him in shock. Others arrived and one of them, Ian Rees, shone his torch at Jumper. The beam keened off the blade.

"Fuck! He's got a knife!" said Ian, real panic in his voice. Jumper aimed the tip of the knife in their direction. Harry's eyes flickered, and he slumped, his breath rattling until the gasps stopped abruptly. Dodger felt for a pulse and there was hardly any, Harry was fatally wounded and going into a convulsion. Dodger tried in vain to find the wound that was pulsing ever less blood from it, but by the time he did, Harry quietly slipped into unconsciousness in his arms. Dodger whipped off Harry's respirator and carefully crawled toward the convulsing Nige and fumbled the mask over his head, his hands wet with fresh blood. Nige coughed a few times, and his breathing recovered, laboriously.

"Any of you fuckers come near me," said Jumper, "… you'll fucking get this!"

"Jumper … you bastard!" screamed Ian through his respirator. "You've fucking-well killed Harry!"

"Your ... fuckin' ... rezzie's over here!" said Dodger who reached over to a drawer and fished out a bag. He tossed it at Jumper who just let it rebound off his legs .

"I fucking mean it!" said Jumper, rage and fear in his voice and everyone believed him.

There was further commotion outside in the lobby, as five more pellets are dropped through the plug in the hatch. Dodger rose, turns and watched through the door the pellets bounced off the steps and the vain attempts to extinguish them. He walked through to the mess square where most people were congregating, and the phone was ringing. He snatched it up.

"Fowler ... FUCK YOU!" he yelled into the mouthpiece.

"Dodger! What's going on?" It was Keith Osbourne.

"Oh! Keith, they're gassing us out!" said Dodger. "The bastards are actually using tear gas on us!"

Keith was horrified. "What? You're joking man!"

Dodger responded, trying to frame his words carefully as he was wearing the respirator. "No, mate. No shit! Harry's dead. Jumper Crossley's stabbed him."

Keith relayed this news to his own messmates. He turned back to Dodger. "Is it Fowler?"

"'Course it is! Him, the rest of the fucking Officers ... the Chiefs and the POs too. They're all kissing his arse because they're all shit scared of him. They're all bastard-well in on it. I fuckin' hate them all." Dodger paused, sobbing. He hoped Keith got all of that. Then he continued, "Listen, shipmate. We'd better do something, and we'd better do it fast. It won't be long before they get bored with us and mosey on down your end. Don't forget – you've got extra lads down there, haven't you? The ones from the messes above? Yeah. I'll bet you a pound-for-a-pinch of shit, they haven't got their gas masks with them, eh?"

Keith knew Dodger was right about this. He had twenty-one extra souls down in his mess now and none of them had their Anti Gas Respirators which were in the messes above. If Fowler started picking on them, what happened to Harry could be a complete bloodbath in his own messdeck. "Yeah," he said. "Good point. We are in shit-street down here." There was an empty pause, which Dodger broke.

"Well, we'd best do summat. I think it's time we took the ship." Keith didn't respond. "I said ... it's time we took the ship over, Keith," Dodger said, again, more slowly this time.

"I know … I know what you said, Dodger," said Keith, trying anything to forget the inevitability in Dodger's suggestion. "I'm just trying to think how we can do it. They've got guns … and now we know they'll fucking use them too!"

"Well, we can't just sit here and take this shit, Keith. If we give up, we will achieve nothing … and it will be a thousand times worse … believe me."

"Hold on, Dodger. I'll give the other messes a ring … see how they feel. I'll talk to Topsy, down the Seaman's mess. He'll be up for it. Sit tight, I'll let you know. Okay?"

"Make it quick, Keith, eh?" said Dodger, and he hung up to allow Keith to get cracking canvassing the other messdecks. Dodger hangs up. He turned round to see three of his messmates dragging Harry's limp, grey-faced body out of the bunk space and into the lobby. Dodger breathed heavily into the respirator.

Chapter Thirteen

1846

Fowler stood with ten other Officers and Senior Ratings in 2 November aft cross passageway drinking coffee from a mug with 'World's Best Husband' on the side of it. The Ops Officer, Lt Cdr Nicholson arrived from up forward.

"Sir ... there's little movement from below in the forward messes," he said, his pasty face damp with sweat and stress. "It looks like they're settling in for the duration. Maybe we should think about contacting them, see what they want to do now ... maybe?"

Fowler looked back at him with disgust and contempt. "No. Not at all. I think a transition phase is taking place ... the misery they are experiencing now will be the trigger for the end of the mutiny, mark my words. It's a mind-game now ... and they are on the back foot, wondering what the hell we are going to try next. It won't be long, you'll see. By twenty-one hundred ... it'll be all over. I'd lay a month's wages on it."

Fowler set himself in thought, then broke out of it. "We should allow some of our men to get some sleep, for now. Post three sentries on each of the hatches to the messdecks and sort out a rota from the Chiefs and POs to supervise. Make sure they are armed. I need to know soonest if any developments arise. I'll be in my cabin." He handed Nicholson his empty cup and turned, disappearing up the port side passageway. Nicholson knew how demeaning this looked, and the Chiefs and Petty Officers present averted their watchful gaze, looking busy out of embarrassment.

One deck below in the Stokers mess it was dark, cold-looking and eerie, with sallow ribbons of CS Gas still hanging at chest-level, illuminated by the gloomy emergency battery-powered lighting. Dodger was on the phone again and most of the mess members were sitting on the seating or the floor of the mess square. All had respirators on. Only one – Jumper Crossley wasn't present. He sat in his gulch with his back against a locker, his knife clasped in his hand. The man he'd murdered earlier lay out in the lobby with two sleeping bags over him.

"Right! Fine! Yeah ... yeah! Did what? I said ... DID WHAT?" Dodger was having problems speaking with the respirator on. "Okay! Nineteen thirty. Yeah … yeah. See you on the outside, boy. Okay? Ciao!" He replaced the receiver and turned to his messmates. A hive of eyepieces locked onto him.

"Fellers … it's on," he announced "Nineteen thirty … Mick, Tanzy, I want you on the ladder at nineteen twenty-five … ready to cut the ropes. Everyone arm themselves with as much weaponry as you can. Nineteen thirty, we cut the ropes, snap open the hatches and hit them, hard. Mac, Colin, Steve and you lot come out of the escape hatch under the sickbay and hit them from the back." People nodded back. No questions. Dodger continued, "Now it's odds-on we'll be rumbled, or they might have their rezzies on as well. So, Topsy, in the Seamen's mess, suggested we wear T-shirts on our heads as bandannas, or summat … so everyone, get yourselves one. We've got thirty-five minutes, lads. Let's fucking do it."

People started to move, getting up, stretching, mobilising. Dodger was impressed how this rabble of thirty or so men, all of them engineers of some sort or ability, could collectively agree to take on this vile authority that had descended upon them, with no clear outcome but trouble upon trouble. He figured after Doc being shot, and the Harry's death, everyone considered they had nothing to lose but small things to gain, even if it was unclear any of them would live through this.

1930

The lobby outside the Stokers mess square and bunk space was packed with men clad in boots, overalls and respirators. All had bandannas of sorts on their heads. Most carried hand weapons, plastic-coated tubes of steel called 'Samson Bars' used to shut hatches, spanners and a few hammers. Someone had a Boston Red Sox baseball bat which was a hangover from a Standing Naval Force Atlantic deployment visit to North America two years ago. Mick and Tanzy stood just under the hatch with knives on the ropes with Dodger just behind them. He looked round. Again, everyone looked up at him like some intense human hive of insects wheezing through their respirators. Many nodded at him. This was gonna fucking happen now. Yes, it fucking was.

"Right! Let's do it," he said, balling his fist. "Quietly, now. Not too much noise. We need to surprise them ..."

Tanzy sliced through the ropes with little sawing movements and Colin gently eased off the catches. They both descended the ladder allowing Atky to ascend followed by three others. They made minimal noise. Atky looked down at Dodger, who looked at his watch again. Dodger slowly lifted his arm which raised the tension, then dropped it suddenly.

The hatch fluidly moved up with Atky underneath it and the sentries, two Petty Officers and a Chief hardly noticed. When it slammed into the keep-clip on the bulkhead, their heads snapped round, startled. Atky stepped off the ladder into the passageway and took two steps toward the first Petty Officer before smacking him directly in the face with his huge right fist. The Petty Officer toppled backwards, sprawling on the deck. A second Petty Officer rose from the deck and shouted, "Shit" at the sight of more Stokers piling out of the mess below and there was a short struggle before control was established. Dodger stood in the centre of the crowd. He whisked off his gasmask, and drew in a deep breath, smiling briefly. Others followed his example and removed theirs too.

Tanzy and Mick had the third Petty Officer held against an electrical cabinet, and the Senior Rate looked terrified. Tanzy drew in close to his face. "Fucking bastard! Expect it was you who put the CS Gas in, was it? Was it? You twat!" Tanzy thumped him low in the guts and the PO crumpled forward, weakly. From further down the spur passageway Keith Osbourne appeared with several others from his mess. Dodger wheeled round to greet him.

"Keith! My man! You okay?"

Keith was pumped. "Yeah! Fuckin' bestial matey!" he cried excitedly, pointing aft where his men were emerging from their own messdeck below and apprehending their sentries. "We dropped four down there. Fucking cunts!" Both moved aft to the messdeck that sat between theirs just as it's hatch swung upward with a bang. From below, Topsy Turner and his mess stared up into the light of the passageway. All had respirators and bandannas on.

"Welcome to the fucking dance, guys," shouted Keith down the hatch. "What took you? Bus late?"

Topsy took off his mask. "You're early! We were gonna …"

"Just get the fuck up here, eh?" called Dodger, and the Seamen's mess started to empty upwards into the passageway. Dodger turned to Ian Rees who was passing.

"Ian, put the lights back on, will you mate? And the ventilation."

Further down the passageway, a group of Seamen arrived outside the Petty Officer's mess and hurtle through the door, taking everyone by complete surprise, whilst another gaggle invaded the POs bunkspace. There, three of them happened across a pre-selected target, asleep in his bunk. They dragged him straight from his bunk onto the deck in his underwear, barely awake and absolutely shitting himself. One of his attackers yelled, "Yes! It's Ruby fucking Murray".

PO Murray cowered in the dark but uttered, "w-wh-what's going on? You will all ... all ... leave this messdeck and report to the Regulating Office. Go on now! That's a direct order!"

Another Seaman yelled down at him, "Shut it! Not so big and clever, now, are you, you fucking prick!" and kicked him square in the chest. Murray fell onto his back, shocked and now angered. He tried vainly to assert some sort of control. "I'm telling you now ... firstly, you ... are in the shit for assault and you two are in the shit for aiding and abetting him."

The first mutineer punched Murray as he tried to rise from his sitting position. Then the other two joined in the assault with more kicks and blows and Murray rolled into a protective ball as they rained in. The third member of this party, the person whose idea it was to single Murray out down below in the mess could see this was getting well out of hand. "C'mon lads. He's had enough," he said, backing off. The other two stopped with Murray now sobbing and gasping. The Petty Officer uncovered his face only for the first Seaman to fire in a kick to his face which, delivered with a steel-toecapped steaming boot did an enormous amount of damage, fracturing his entire upper jaw and nose area and eye sockets, pushing it backwards into his brain. A copious amount of blood erupted from Murray's mouth, nose and eyes. He slumped forward and lapsed into unconsciousness already close to death, his short breaths rattly and gurgling. All three mutineers witnessed this, looked at each other briefly and backed toward the door, leaving Murray to die on the carpet of his own naval messdeck, six thousand miles from home.

In the cross-passageway above the Stokers mess people were congregating. All had bandannas on, some stripped to the waist with their overalls tied about their midriffs by the arms. Dodger climbed onto the bottom steps of a ladder leading upwards and waved his hands to silence the rabble.

"Fellers! Fellers!" he shouted "Listen! Hey!" A crowd of about fifty men silenced gradually to a low babble. Heads gradually turned toward him. Dodger continued, "Right, lads! We don't have long … so I'll be brief. We've done the hardest part of this … so now it's a mutiny …"

There was a murmur of discontentment mixed with jubilation, Dodger couldn't tell which, but he ignored it for now. "… lads … please! Right. Thank-you. It is a mutiny … and we now must finish the whole meal, or we will be in a worse world of shit than ever."

"So, what we gonna do, then?" came a Welsh accented voice, identity unknown.

Dodger jumped in, trying to maintain momentum. "Well, I reckon the best thing to do is to split up. We can then move along 2 deck and take it, section-by-section. The whole nine-yards. Ops Room, Machinery Control Room, everything. Them lot up top will be snookered. We will have control of the ship. We can call the shots. We can also see how the Radio Operators and Gunners are up forward …"

Somone japed, "Probably still got their fucking heads down," which raised a titter. It was something Dodger realised he had to latch onto. "First thing we want," he said "… above anything, is Fowler off this ship. The WEO can take charge until we get along side in East Cove in the Falklands." People tended to agree with this. It seemed reasonable. "Then we want no comeback on this … no-one gets in the shit, yeah? Not one of us …"

"Fuckin' chance of that … eh? We're all in the shit! No exceptions!" John Fisher called out in an exasperated manner.

Topsy shot him down dismissively, "Shut it, you jobless prick! We'll say what's what! It's our fucking ship now!" A larger cheer broke out, mainly from those present from Topsy's own mess and Dodger was grateful for his assistance. He continued, "Once we've got 2 deck, we can negotiate. We'll rope shut the machinery space escape hatches so they can't get in." Dodger looked round at the sailors before him and took a deep breath. "From 2 deck down … we'll own the ship."

Chapter Fourteen

2021

On *Warwick's* Bridge, Officer of the Watch Lt Dean Driscoll and Petty Officer 'Spud' Murphy kept vigil, Murphy standing in for both Quartermaster and Boatswain's Mate both of whom were now part of the mutiny, one of whom had meted out some of the pasting to Petty Officer Ruby Murray down aft a few minutes ago on account of shared hatred of him as a rather tyrannical part of ship PO. Driscoll wasn't a man of much conversation, and both had really run out of things to say about this rather frightening and unusual situation. Neither of them knew of the messdeck breakout down aft too. The ship was still on track, course 220 and at 14 knots being driven by one Tyne engine with the other shaft trailing, to conserve fuel. Driscoll moseyed over to the 'Conning 1' station and picked up the microphone.

"Plot, Bridge," he said. Three decks below in the equally darkened Operations Room, Petty Officer Taff Richards sat at the navigation radar plot, again subbing for an absent Leading Hand whose job it actually was. Boy, was he fucked off with this.

"Plot," said Richards, disinterestedly.

"What's the … er … closest contact and CPA?"

"Standby," said Richards, and scanned the three running radars. The 1022 long range D Band radar went out to over 200 miles.

"Bridge, Plot," said Richards into his microphone.

"Bridge," responded Driscoll.

"No contacts to report. We're clear out and beyond all radars." Richards sounded resentful and huffy. Driscoll looked over at Murphy who sipped his coffee and looked straight forward into the southern Atlantic, now starting to gust a little.

"Very good," said Driscoll. He felt very alone, confused, tired and vulnerable. His training hadn't prepared him for this stuff.

In the centre of 2 deck, the Machinery Control Room sat above the two main engine rooms, centrally controlling and surveying the propulsion and services equipment and systems that kept *Warwick* moving and alive. Chief of the Watch was Petty Officer Brian Szchupak and sat on the engine Propulsion Control Levers and his second in charge was Petty Officer Billy Durrant, who'd joined the ship just prior to sailing and was a relative new face around the Marine Engineers. Nevertheless, the conversation was ripe and speculative regarding the mutiny.

"Fowler says that we'll be chucking more CS down the messes at 2100. Says that it'll flush the fuckers out." Durrant placed both his steaming boots on the sill of the panel and slunk in his chair.

"Don't give a shit," retorted Szchupak, dismissively. "S'long as I don't get hurt in this …fuck 'em. Little bastards! What kind of fucking Navy do they think it is, anyway?" He leant forward and the HQ1 PO, standing in the doorway leant in also. "Cah! I know who it is, y'know! I could name 'em all, right now."

The sliding door to the MCR from 2 deck opened and five overall-clad men burst through. Atky, leading the group, had a small wooden baton, and held it in front of Szcupak's shocked face.

"Gentlemen," said Atky. "This way if you don't fucking mind." Both Petty Officers were forced to their feet and led aft to their mess where the rest of the POs were corralled, and Colin Parsons took over as Chief of the Watch. In reality, he had no idea what the fuck he was doing.

Further forward on 2 deck, PO Taff Richards heard the Ops Room door slide open behind in the darkness. This had better be his fucking relief because he was not happy with having to do Plot watches again, no siree. He turned and saw Topsy Turner and other Junior Ratings striding toward him. Richards snatched up the microphone and blurted, "Bridge, Plot!" Just then Topsy smacked him in the face with a straight left, toppling him over in his chair. The microphone fell from his grasp and swung bouncing from its black, coiled wire.

"Bridge!" called Driscoll, hoping it was something, anything of nearby shipping because right now, he was not feeling too good about anything.

Topsy picked up the microphone. "Bridge, Plot. Disregard," he said.

Elsewhere on 2 deck more Chief and Petty Officers were being rounded up and manhandled aft to the Petty Officer's mess. One of these, the Chief Weapons Electrician was desperately pleading with Dodger, clad only in his voluminous boxer shorts and flip-flops. His head was oozing blood from a nasty connection with a locker as he was dragged bodily from his bunk by two lads.

"Dodger ... look, mate. Dodger! For God's sake!" he said, almost blubbing. "Don't let the bastards hurt us, eh? We don't want any trouble. Just tell us what to do, yeah? We'll give you no hassle! Please!"

Dodger placed the Samson Bar down on an electrical cabinet and put his hand on the Chief's shoulder. "Oh, it's okay, Chief. Just go aft with the rest of them and you'll be all right," he said, reassuringly.

"... please! Don't let ... 'em ... hurt me! Look! I don't want to ... *please*!" he begged back.

"This way, fat boy. Please," said Keith Osbourne, prodding a night stick into the Chief's flabby midriff. He led him aft and forcefully pushed him through the POs Mess door. Somewhere in the background a phone was beeping and Tanzy picked it up. A hush lowered the noise level to a murmur. "Yeah?" said Tanzy. His face went from indignation to mild amusement as the person on the other end relayed the news.

"Right," Tanzy said and replaced the receiver. He turned to Dodger and Keith, who'd just returned. "2 deck is ours!"

Mild, contained celebrations went on with small fist displays and air punches. This was a minor triumph over Fowler.

Les Tremayne emerged from his cabin, moving aft through the officer's cabin flat where the rest of the Heads of Department are billeted. He descended one ladder and then went to descend the one below onto 2 deck only to find it shut. He stared blankly at the hatch top. All the clips were in the engaged position. He went to move one and something cold licked the base of his heart. It was rigid. It had been put on with purpose and secured. He crossed the passageway past the Commanding Officer's cabin and over to the opposite side of the ship where a hatch led downward to the Operations Room. That too was shut, and the handles solidly applied.

The Ops Officer appeared. "What's up?"

"Hmmm ..." said Tremayne. "These hatches. Has XO ... um CO ordered them shut for any reason?"

"Not that I'm aware of," said Nicholson. The penny seemed to drop quickly. "Hang on …" he said.

"Yeah," said Tremayne. "The other side is shut too. We've got problems. Big fucking problems."

They climbed the ladder above the hatch and walk back to the Captain's Cabin, where Fowler sat in an easy chair, reading Jane's Fighting Ships. WEO knocked the door. Fowler looked up.

"Yes? Do come in, man!" he said, quite cheerily considered the situation. "What's the news? Finally given up, have they?"

Tremayne and Nicholson stepped in. A half-downed bottle of scotch whiskey sat on the desk.

"No, sir. All the hatches to 2 deck have been roped shut," Tremayne explained. "Someone … or more correctly something is holding them closed. There's little we can do. We can't get into the Ops Room at all."

On 2 deck, both port and starboard passageways feed into central compartments, one of which is the relatively spacious Junior Ratings Dining Hall, now with the chairs stacked and the four-man tables folded up against the bulkheads and clipped. Ten minutes after Fowler had the bad news related to him regarding being cut off from 2 deck, Dodger had made a call round the Junior Ratings messdecks and had most of them assembled before him. Those missing were the volunteers guarding the Chiefs and Petty Officers down aft, and the two chefs apprehended in the raid on their mess which resulted in Doc Savage's death. Even Toby Faulkner, earlier missing in the outbreak, had re-emerged. Dodger tried to make his five-foot ten frame taller to get his voice over the heads of the men before him. All were still wearing overalls; some still had their bandanna headgear on. The men looked dirty, dishevelled and tired, however there was excited babble.

Dodger waved and the crowd shushed itself quiet. "Okay … chaps! We now have the whole of 2 deck …" to which a muted, if enthusiastic cheer came back at him. Some fists were raised, triumphantly. The men started to babble again. Dodger tried to wrestle order back a bit.

"… Okay … ha … right! Listen … fellers! Please!" he said, and the crowd quietened a bit.

"… right … then. What we're gonna do is … er … at twenty-two hundred, we'll knock off the electrics to the bridge, shut down the steering system and take the engines into MCR control. Then we'll stop the ship in the water."

Topsy cut in, loudly and garrulously. "Hold on a bit, Dodger! Why don't we just take the fucking lot, eh? We've come this far … and there's enough of us. I say we finish the job!" he looked round, largely at the gaggle of his own men nearby. "Take the lot off 'em! I've done this before, I tell you. No way I'm fucking having that again." Men beside him and others further afield started nodding.

Dodger didn't need this. "Topsy, look …" he began.

"Yeah! Let's break open the small arms. Dish out the fucking guns," said a man next to Topsy.

"Fucking mooch. And the pistols," said another Able Seaman.

"Let's *do* the bastards!" said a third, and the meeting again descended into a rebellious parliament. Topsy started up a chant which gained a foothold.

"Kill the bastards! Kill the bastards! Kill the bastards …"

Dodger tried to talk over this, desperately clawing this away from where it was heading. "Lads! Please! Look …! Look …I know that … please, listen! Lads … I know that they're all tooled up … yeah. But the last thing we need right now is twenty or thirty hotheads prowling round the ship loosing off rounds from high powered rifles. For Christ's sake, fellers!" He looked around, trying to get everyone's eye, imploring them to ratchet it down a notch at least. "We're all in the shit, now ... all of us! Even them lot will stand from under when the brass in Whitehall get to know about this!"

"You're in the shit, pal," said Fisher, sarcastically and flatly.

"It's not what we're after, is it? All we want is justice ... eh?" Dodger could tell he was losing this already. "We all want Fowler out. Don't we?"

Topsy wasn't bought. "No! Fuck them, I say! Fuck them all! Do the twats! They will have us all, if we don't! Dodger, just think ... them cunts shot Doc Savage ... if we give in, we're fucked!" Again, the assembled crowd were more in agreement with Topsy's vision. Dodger was worried and desperate.

"No, Topsy! Let's just stop the ship ... and see what happens." This was met with barracking and calls of 'no!' from the men.

"Who put you in charge, anyway?" said Fisher. Dodger chose to ignore it.

"Look. For fuck's sake! We've all got to pull in the same direction, here. This isn't Beirut or the Bronx, for fuck's sake. If we don't get it together, Fowler fucking-well wins ..." he stepped off the chair and exited the Dining Hall, casting an icy stare toward Topsy and Fisher. A low babble emanated again from the sailors as they dispersed.

2204

Fowler held a framed photograph of Cdr Stuart Belmont's wife in his hands, sat at the Captain's desk in his cabin. He looked longingly at the woman in the picture, a typical English Rose and naval wife. Fowler wondered if she had a penchant for rough, Junior Rating's dicks or if Belmont deservedly slapped her about a bit like he had Colleen at times. It seemed not. In this awkward silence and across the cabin sat Ops Officer Bob Nicholson mostly in darkness, quietly contemplating his own slaying of a tubby Leading Chef a few hours ago and wondering now how the fuck he'd get away with that come the enquiry. The phone beeped on

Belmont's desk and the stand-in Captain of *Warwick* picked up the receiver.

"Captain," he said. The Officer of the Watch was on the other end.

"Sir. Officer of the Watch," said Driscoll, who had now been on watch on the Bridge for what seemed too long. "The ship is failing to respond to telegraph and lever orders and is slowing down. We have lost way of the ship. The Machinery Control Room is not replying to any contact, sir!"

"Speed?" said Fowler.

"Four knots," came the reply.

"Bearing?"

"Ah, er … yes sir, continued Driscoll. "Both gyrocompasses have just failed. Alarms are up. Fail set bearing is … well … the rudder is hard-to starboard. We are just passing three-two-zero. The steering gear is not responding. Satellite navigation is down. The panel's dead. Even our navigation lights are dead."

"I'll be in the wardroom. Take a fix by the stars and get me the ship's position. Run a check on what we have available and let me know soonest."

"Aye, sir!" said Driscoll.

"Good man," replied Fowler.

Fowler slammed the phone down in fury and the handset hook and receiver shatter under the force. Fowler's finger split and blood oozed out. Fowler turned round and faced Nicholson.

"Think it's time to talked to the men," he said casually and slugged the half glass of scotch straight down, then with a facial grimace and an "aaaaaah," replaced the glass on Belmont's desk, blood still dripping from his hand.

Chapter Fifteen

2255

Topsy was busy handing out eight Browning semi-automatic handguns to various people in his trust in the passageway above the Stoker's mess, plus magazines and handfuls of lethal, squat, purposeful-looking 9mm rounds. Dodger held one also and it felt weird. This wasn't dropped hatches anymore and it wasn't simple disobedience and rebellion. They were now tooled up for internal armed combat, and Dodger wasn't that happy. According to Topsy, six Brownings were missing from the armoury up forward as well as six L1A1 Self Loading Rifles, two shotguns and two specialist snipers' rifles, complete with nightscopes. This meant someone else had these upstairs and there was now a greater possibility more people might be killed. Dodger tried to supress the fear it might be him and he thought, but tried not to, of his mum, his sister and finally of Louise. Topsy removed the gun from his grasp, slid in a full magazine and gave it back to him with a grin, reaching inside his top overalls pocket and fishing out a packet of Embassy Regal, flicking open the lid and shaking it to offer Dodger one. Dodger took it and lit it from Topsy's own cigarette and enjoyed the luxury of the respiratory burn.

"Cheers, buddy," he said and went and sat on the handle of a damage control salvage pump, watching the proceedings. Suddenly the main broadcast clicked, static, clicked off, then clicked on again.

"Fellers!" shouted Ian Rees. "Sssssh! Shit-in-it! Sssssssh!" People quietened their gossip again.

Fowler's voice cut through the speaker. "Right … ah. D'yer hear there! I wish to meet with all members of this insurrection which is happening in certain isolated areas of the ship. Leading Hands of Messdecks should attend, also. Muster, on the flightdeck at midnight. The flightdeck lights will be switched on … and … we will be unarmed." Topsy glanced across at Dodger and shook his head.

Fowler continued, "I will be lenient with my judgements and supportive, within reason, to any suggestions or demands. That is all."

Tanzy stopped what he was doing and looked up at the speaker on the bulkhead. "Yeah! How's about 'Go fuck yourself!'?" he called.

Dodger was still looking at Topsy. Keith was looking at both of them in deadlock.

"It's a trap, Dodger," said Topsy "I'm telling you!" Dodger stood up and looked away. He felt wretched and sick. He also felt afraid. Topsy's words – 'it's a trap' – ricocheted around in his brain. What was he to do? Go with Topsy and possibly further the violence, or meet with Fowler and come to some, any agreement that may or may not end up with Fowler still running the ship and everyone suffering? Or end up being shot or kicked to death like that Petty Officer they'd just bodily dragged out and thrown from the quarterdeck into the Atlantic on Topsy's orders? Either way, they were well in this now. Nothing happy or pleasing was up ahead. And he was mostly responsible. He turned to the gaggle of people who had gathered and were looking to him for an executive decision, one he now knew his fouled anchor didn't qualify him to make. It was time to think on your feet, the thought, but even that made him shit himself. One thing was certain, with Harry now dead and also being bound up for some sort of burial down in 3 November, he wasn't courageous enough to go upstairs onto the flightdeck and talk Fowler down.

"Okay. What we need is seven volunteers. We dress them in overalls, Rezzies and antiflash. We make sure they don't know who they are." Dodger held up a pistol. "We give them one of these each. If anything happens, we back them up. Yeah?" It sounded baseless, cowardly and weak, but it was the best he could offer.

Topsy stood up, angrily. "Oh yeah. And how do you suppose we get the volunteers? Pay 'em?"

Dodger moved past him, slapping a hand on his shoulder, "Don't know, shippers. Use your fucking charm. If we go up there and they get us, then this is over." He descended the ladder into 3 November mess lobby, if only to get himself out of the firing line. He also needed to corral some twerp into going up top in lieu of himself. Atky was supervising a mess clean up, sat on the bar top, smoking what looked like a joint. Tanzy stood leaning on the Henry vacuum cleaner lance, talking to anyone.

"… and …" he said, "… I bet they send us all back to the UK when we get to the Falklands."

No one seemed to be taking much notice. Everyone collectively felt knackered, mentally and physically. Dodger passed Tanzy, waiting for anyone to pick the thread of his conversation up and headed for Ian Rees, collecting used cups in a bucket.

"Shippers," he said, putting his hand round Ian's shoulders. Ian straightened up, with a suspicious look on his face.

"Can I have a word?" Dodger nodded his head sideways, toward the bunkspace. Ian followed Dodger into the end gulch, still carrying the bucket of cups.

"Yeah?" said Ian.

"Would you go up to the flightdeck?" Ian tiled his head to one side and smiled.

"Yeah mate. Sure, I will!" he said smiling. Then his face went serious. "Fuck off."

"No, look. Hold on … it's no problem. We'll get you a pistol …" This sounded desperate. And it was.

"… but they're unarmed," said Ian. Dodger could tell, he was losing this.

"Yeah, I know. Just in case, eh? Just talk to them. We need Fowler out. I don't give a shit who gets the job ... but not him, right?"

"Just talk to him, yeah?" said Ian, smiling again. "No hot stuff?"

"Yeah," said Dodger. "Yeah. C'mon, eh? Uckers champion. International superstar ..."

Ian's face dropped again. "And my dick's a chocolate éclair. Bite it, eh? No offence, but just piss off, pal, yeah? You started all of this. You do the fucking negotiations. Count me out."

Tanzy, who clearly had been listening to most of this moseyed past, pulling the Henry. "I wouldn't do it, Ian. No way."

"I'm fucking not," Ian snorted and barged past Dodger, cups clinking in the bucket.

"I'll do it," came a voice from the next gulch. It was Jumper Crossley. "Got fuck-all to lose, have I? I mean ... I've fucking stabbed Harry. You're all gonna fucking stitch me up when we get to the fucking Falklands, anyway. I don't mind. I'll fucking do it."

Dodger and Tanzy exchanged uneasy looks. Tanzy's eyes widened and he raised his eyebrows.

"No … er, thanks, Jumper and all that," said Dodger, weakly. "I think I need one of the Leading Hands for this. Cheers … all the same."

"Suit your fucking selves," replied Jumper, indignantly. Dodger hoped it wouldn't trigger him into some sort of continuation of his stabbing spree.

Steve Hepplethwaite bumbled in, breathlessly, edging past Tanzy on his way to his locker.

"Steve," said Dodger. "Favour to ask, me old mate."

"For you sweetcheeks," Steve replied, "the fucking world …"

2345

Petty Officer Crawford stooped and felt with his hands amongst the angular apparatus on top of *Warwick's* helicopter hangar in the darkness of the South Atlantic night. By the very bright stars in the clear skies, he could tell the ship had its bow pointing at ninety degrees to the gentle breeze, which was laden with damp and cold. Fortunately, the sea had calmed somewhat, and the ship wasn't rolling and pitching too much, but he could tell they were a long, long way from anywhere because the horizon was barely visible. Below him he could however make out the outline of the flightdeck and its rounded extremities, as well as the white markings on the deck with the letters WK stencilled near the stern. Crawford found a decent spot and settled, slightly to the port side. He'd brought a tarpaulin up from the Top Part of Ship Locker and threw it round himself. Then he thumbed the ON/OFF toggle on the AN/PVS-4 Night Vision scope and hauled the American-built M21 rifle it was fitted to up to his shoulder. Through the scope the flightdeck was entirely visible down to the bolts retaining the arrester nets along the periphery. He zeroed the aimpoint in on the reticule, swung the rifle up and picked out the glowing body of an albatross swinging its way across the stern in the eddy winds. Crawford switched the scope off, blew on his hands and pulled the cover right over him.

Seven and hundred and fifty metres off the starboard quarter the Spanish Naval Submarine *Siroco* lowered its periscope.

Inside the silent, scarlet-lit control room the Commanding Officer spoke to order the helmsman to change course.

"Course, zero, zero five, sir. Three knots," the helmsman replied.

"Three knots," repeated the Captain.

"What's happening?" asked the Operations Officer, sipping coffee.

"Nothing ... nothing at all," shrugged the Captain. "They are drifting, with their lights off, apparently uncontrolled. Even their radars are not moving or transmitting. They can't have broken down. We would have had a distress call by now, surely."

"Wonder if NATO HQ are aware?" mused the Executive Officer.

The Captain paused, deep in thought. "We'll wait until dawn and then contact them. This is most irregular. Position the boat on her starboard beam and come to periscope depth. I need to look at her Bridge ..."

The submarine dived thirty metres and silently steamed astern of *Warwick*, gliding under the stationary warship, positioning itself five hundred metres abeam of her thirty-five minutes later. Ten metres below the surface the periscope popped up again. *Warwick* had swung about in the wind so presented her starboard quarter to *Siroco*. The Captain ordered twenty revolutions on her propellor shaft to move the submarine forward, then suddenly called 'Alto!'

The flightdeck illumination lights used for night flying bathed the flightdeck in pools of light. Crawford peeped out from the tarpaulin and witnessed the circular hatch at the extreme aft end of the flight-deck lift. A hand peeped out from its rim and a blue-overall clad figure climbed the ladder, up from the quarterdeck below. He was clad in an anti-flash hood with a respirator on. Another man appeared, then another, until seven figures stood in a broad arc at the rear of the ship. No real clues gave Crawford who was stood on the flightdeck, but they all appeared to be Leading Hands, hopefully of the individual messdecks that had mutinied. Fowler's plan was explained an hour ago to him and several others that he was going to decapitate the insurrection by capturing the ringleaders. If there was any resistance or sign of violence, he had Fowler's permission to 'take them out of the game'. When Fowler said this, he nodded at the M21 slung over Crawford's shoulder. Both men had no objection to this. Lt Cdr Tremayne however, who had reluctantly volunteered to join Fowler's snatch squad rolled his eyes when Fowler issued his ad hoc Rules of Engagement to his Petty Officer and hoped they would all come quietly. Something told him they wouldn't.

Across the flightdeck facing the mutineers the hangar door slowly raised, being wound upward by someone within. The interior of the hangar remained dark and empty without the helicopter but people moving about within could be seen by the seven men. Fowler suddenly stepped forward from the shadows into the light and walked alone, halfway across the flightdeck. He stopped and beckoned the seven mutineers forward. The men move forward ten metres when Fowler holds up his hands.

"That's far enough!" he yelled, and the mutineers stopped in a line, a metre between each man.

"So, I take it you are the leaders of this sorry spectacle?" he called out over the breeze. No answer came back. Fowler put his hands on his hips. "Well? What is it you want?"

Steve Hepplethwaite stepped forward a pace. "We want you off this ship, you fucking tosser!" he said, pointing at Fowler.

"I don't think that is an issue, frankly. Besides, it's not at all possible. I run this ship. Now do as I say, and no-one will get hurt. Go below, and call off your stupidity, before …"

Suddenly an Able Seaman from Topsy's messdeck gestured aggressively, "No way! You … can fuck right off! We want you out. The Ops officer or the WEO can run things. We don't want you. You're a cunt!"

Up over their heads, Crawford zeroed his scope on the right eyepiece of this man's respirator. He gently clicked off the safety catch and moved his index finger inside the trigger-guard, settling his breathing as he did so. His tongue prodded out of his mouth slightly and he relaxed his body.

Fowler shot back at the Able Seaman, and then to all the men facing him. "Unfortunately, the codes of military discipline don't allow for such populist horseshit, sonny. We don't run things by ballot box in this man's fucking Navy. Understand?"

The men remained silent and unmoved.

"So, I take that as a refusal, eh?"

"Aint that the fucking truth!" yelled the mutineer of the extreme right of the group.

Fowler stared at them contemptuously for a moment, then turned toward the hangar. "As you wish," he said.

As he reached the shadows, four Officers and two Chief Petty Officers quickly appeared from the darkness, all carrying rifles, and immediately took up position, aiming directly at the mutineers. The mutineers immediately panicked, broke up and backed off, some with their hands held aloft. The Able Seaman hastily reached inside his overall pocket for his pistol. As he attempted to yank it free, the cocking lever snagged on the upper side of his pocket, and he stalled to free it. Crawford's sights came back on target, and he squeezed the trigger. The round blew off a large portion of the Able Seaman's head, and he fell straight to the deck. The errant body part took off in the wind and splashed into the sea some distance astern, becoming supper for the hungry albatross.

Another mutineer, once the firing had commenced, dived for cover and the several others fled back toward the hatch at the back of the flightdeck. The covering mutineer was shot by one of the Chiefs in the confusion. Just two mutineers remained standing with their arms held up, both trembling and yelling with terror. Crawford rose to a kneeling position and continued firing at the escapees, queuing to descend the hatch. One looked up at him and caught a round in the ribs, which chopped out a large chunk of tissue. He reeled against the guardrails and coughed before falling forward. This accelerated the descent of the ladder, the final man falling bodily down it and the hatch slammed shut and locked before the following Officers could reach it. Two bodies lay crumpled on the rough deck surface, one dead and the other oozing his last out as everything went dark.

Fowler walked out into the spotlights where the remaining mutineers are still standing, rigid. He approached one and painfully whisked off his respirator. The man was sobbing, terrified. Fowler kneed him in hard the testicles and he choked to the deck.

Fowler turned and walked back to the hanger. "I want them both in my cabin under armed guard in five minutes," he said to the Officers and Senior Ratings present. The mutineers were bundled onto their feet and led away.

Directly beneath the flightdeck one deck down only five Junior Ratings guarded the thirty-six Chief and Petty Officer captives sat in their own spacious mess. The prisoners sat mainly on the floor and seating area with three Juniors stood by the door and two behind the bar. The gunfire above them could be clearly heard, as could the clatter of rounds ricochetting off the flightdeck. Outside in the passageway a commotion and confusion started to build with panicked, raised voices being heard. The guards looked uneasy and shiftily at each other and two raised their Browning pistols where they could be seen more clearly.

"Easy, fellers," said one in a falsely calm manner. The Senior Ratings assembled, themselves exchanged furtive glances. The tension built considerably.

One of the guards exited through the door to see what was going on. Steve Hepplethwaite had arrived from the Quarterdeck where two of the negotiators were being treat from gunshot wounds. One of them had a round that had travelled straight through his thigh, and he was pumping blood through the wound as those who'd gone to help applied pressure. Steve met with Dodger and Topsy in the aft cross passageway. His face was white with shock, and he was gasping and sobbing, having just escaped with his own life. He slumped forward against an electrical panel and vomited, beige, watery tea trickling out onto the deck. Steve them fell backward and caught sight of Dodger who was almost paralysed with fear and foreboding.

"… fuck … fuckin' … aw … God! Shit, Dodger! They shot some of 'em. Richy, Smudge…I think … someone else's been … shot, too!" Steve struggled to get another breath back in. "They just came at us. F … !"

"Fowler?" completed Topsy, angrily. Steve nodded back and started to sob, uncontrollably, like a little boy. He slumped down breathlessly to a seated position. The guards moved out of the PO's mess into the passageway joined the gathering crowd, leaving a solitary man with the pistol to watch the captives. This was the signal the Senior Ratings needed, and they rushed the man, instantly overpowering him. More Senior Rates spilled out into the passageway. There then commenced a fierce, desperate fist fight between many men as the struggle for power and control continued. It abated slightly when mutineer reinforcements arrived in force and the Seniors were themselves, swamped and overcome. Topsy raised his Browning above the heads of the brawl, chambered a round, knocked off the safety catch and fired it twice into a rack of four-inch Damage Control timber just above his head. The crack from the gun stopped everyone, almost like a video pause-button. There were many casualties, blood splattered on the deck and fittings and some bodies lying motionless. The Senior Rates were raised and restrained then herded, some struggling and receiving further punishment, back to the PO's mess. Dodger had backed off from the action, but had still received a few blows, and was seated, gasping, leaning upon one elbow. Topsy broke away from shoving a Petty Officer to one side and rounded on Dodger.

"You fucking wanker! You trusted them!" He walked over and kicked Dodger in the face in pure anger. Dodger reeled back in shock at this violent outburst. Topsy then rained in a few token blows. Then he backed off.

"You're a fucking prick!" he screamed down at Dodger. "I've got the ship, now! I'll tell you this, shithead. All these twats are in the fucking liferafts, first thing tomorrow! We're gonna slay them for this, just you fucking watch us!"

Dodger tried to rise, still stunned by the kick to his face. "No, Topsy! You can't do that! Don't do it!" he shouted.

Topsy swung round raised the pistol and ranged it four inches from Dodger's face, the safety catch still off and a round still in the chamber. Dodger could smell the cordite from the barrel. "You gonna fucking stop us? Huh? Fuck you! These cunts don't fight fair! I'll fucking show em!"

Chapter Sixteen

East Cove Naval Facility, Mare Harbour, Falkland Islands
Monday 3rd October 1988
0822

East Cove Naval Facility is a purpose-built stone and concrete jetty with warehousing run by the RAF Port Authority prodding out into Mare Harbour on East Falkland, some twenty miles by rough roads from the capital, Port Stanley. A better service road leads directly north to the newly built RAF Mount Pleasant Airfield complex which now serves as the Falkland Islands main military hub with flights now arriving daily from the UK via Ascension Island and a squadron of F1 Tornadoes and C130K Hercules as a handy deterrent for any future ambitions of their nearby neighbours.

The Royal Fleet Auxiliary tanker, *White Rover* backed slowly out of her berth in front of the warship *HMS Athene*, an Exocet-armed Leander-class frigate. *Athene* had been on station as Atlantic Patrol Ship (South) for five months and her ships company eagerly awaited the welcome sight of the Type 42 Destroyer *HMS Warwick* appearing round the headland so they could return home to Devonport, via a courtesy visit to Salvador de Bahia in Brazil and Madeira.

As he glided past the ageing and weather-battered warship, *White Rover's* captain, Desmond Slack was stood watching the Officer of the Watch and overseeing the proceedings from the bridge wing. His own First Lieutenant, Fitz Latham, approached.

"All well, sir?" said the second-in-command.

Slack turned slightly, "Yes. Any word from *Warwick*, yet?"

"Not a squeak," said Latham. "I expect we'll hear from them sometime this forenoon. HQ haven't heard, either."

"Really? That's most unusual." Slack turned back to look out over the harbour, "Well…they'd better get a bloody move on … if they want refuelling, that is."

"'Expect they're looking forward to *Warwick* arriving so they can fuck off home for Christmas," said Latham, nodding toward *Athene*.

"Yeah. Me too. I was down here all last Christmas. It was fucking bleak and miserable I can tell you." Slack paused, watching events on *Athene's* fo'c'sle. "They're just loading on more 4.5 rounds before they go."

They both watched this as the Officer of the Watch swung the stern round to slow the tanker and have its bow facing the South Atlantic through the harbour mouth. Slack turned and made toward the Bridge door. Holding it open he said, "If you hear anything … I'll be in my cabin."

Eleven hundred miles northeast of the Falkland Islands, *Warwick* lazily rolled without propulsion in a gathering swell, beam-on to the waves. Every ten or so minutes a large South Atlantic roller would heave the ship over making its occupants brace against anything solid, before flicking back across its longitudinal and lateral vertical axes. Inside every one of these beings, mutineer or not, existed a finely tuned internal gyroscope which simply ignored this instability and planted feet and centres of gravity appropriately to counter any wave action from the ship. As humans, we'd been doing it for millennia.

On *Warwick's* Bridge Lt Driscoll was back on station as Officer of the Watch after eight hours of fitful, unrewarding sleep. He hadn't had a shower either as those little bastards downstairs had switched off the water and was missing his run round the upper deck. Even the shithouses were backed up, mainly because Ian Rees had closed the valves which carried the sewage outlets from the Officers heads down to the treatment plants. Everything was fragmenting, badly and he prayed order would be restored and fucking soon. Across the Bridge on the helm sat Petty Officer Crawford, pretty much unemployed as steering and engine control had been taken into local control and his binnacle was just reading back the ships heading as it slewed with the wind. Just to his left, the VHF short range radio popped and crackled. Then a voice burst out from it.

"Warship *Warwick* … warship *Warwick* …" The accent was definitely Spanish inflected with the 'r's bounced, and *'Warwick'* pronounced 'War-week'.

Driscoll looked over at Crawford who looked back, almost for once in a startled manner. Driscoll crossed the Bridge and picked up the hand-held microphone. "Yes … this is *Warwick*, over. Who are you? Identify yourself please …" There was a pause of static, which raised both their suspicions.

Suddenly the radio answered. "Warship *Warwick*. This is … ah … er … Spanish Naval Submarine … *Siroco*. Do you … ah … having trouble, there? Over … "

Driscoll dropped the microphone to his side and looked at Crawford. "Argentine?" the Petty Officer said. Driscoll shrugged.

"Where's *Jane's Fighting Ships*?" he said to Crawford. Every Bridge on every British warship carried a copy. He wanted to check the identity of this 'submarine'. His background knowledge of Spanish Naval vessels was practically non-existent. As *Warwick's* Fighter Control officer however, he had vast intelligence on the capability of the Argentine Air Force's capability. Driscoll keyed the handset, "What is your current position, *Siroco*? Over …"

After another short pause, the radio responded again. "I am … ah … about seven kilometre to your … port quarter. Are you … ah … having a difficulty, *Warwick*?"

Driscoll replied cautiously. "Erm … negative *Siroco*." They'd obviously been watching the ship for some time. The last thing he wanted to do was inform the Argentines they were right in the middle of a crew insurrection.

"You have been adrift for some times now," said the radio. "Hah! I ... hoping things all okay, now. Ah, erm, over."

Driscoll paused, trying to get a response that sounded reassuring and not panicky. "Yes, thanks for your concern. Over." He winced. That sounded shit.

"Warship *Warwick*," the submarine said. "We, er, obser ... observing ... gun ... fire on your helicop-i-ter deck, last night. Over." Driscoll's face drained of blood, and he felt cold and breathless. He reached across to Crawford who was quickly flipping through a 1979 version of *Jane's Fighting Ships*. "Get the Skipper, now!"

Crawford snatched up his rifle from beside the Quartermaster's console. Suddenly there was the sound of shouting and commotion from the hatch at the back of the Bridge. He backed away from the hatch. One deck down mutineers had finally broken out from down below and were brutalising the remaining Officers in their cabins. Their torture could clearly be heard from the Bridge and Topsy and a few of his men slowly ascended the ladder to the Bridge, menacingly, bandannas on their heads, guns in their hands and menace in their faces. Crawford picked up some binoculars and his foul weather jacket and stealthily slipped out of the Bridge wing door unnoticed, out onto the upperdeck, leaving Driscoll transfixed in horror. The Officer of the Watch raised the microphone to his mouth and spoke, "*Siroco*, this is *Warwick*. We have a serious situation here. We have crew insurrection, and a mutiny is taking place. We need help. The mutineers are armed, and we have had many deaths. Please contact NATO headquarters at Northwood, ASAP. Out."

Just as he said 'out', Topsy drove the butt of his Self-Loading Rifle into Driscoll's face, breaking his jaw and taking out six of his teeth.

Dodger lay in his bunk in his overalls and boots on top of his sleeping bag, staring at the deckhead above him some twenty inches away. His bunklight was on and he looked sideways and removed the picture of the girl on the motorcycle from its Blutak tethers and stared longingly at her. Before *Warwick* left on this deployment, he'd been with her in a hotel in Andover, not far from where she lived. Everything about that weekend was so damned right, and he finally felt she was 'the one'. He also felt secure enough she'd be there for him during the soulless days until his return and maybe … hopefully …

forever. He'd had shorter relationships before her, but some time drying out after the Falklands War and ongoing behavioural and attitude problems ended them abruptly. His mum always said, 'you'll meet the one you marry when you won't be looking for her' and in a way she was right. Louise had simply dropped from high above out of nowhere and after fifteen months this was their first big test. Now Dodger wasn't even sure if, when or how he'd see her again. As he looked on her image his throat closed up with emotion and he tried to suppress a sob but couldn't. She was possibly at home right now at her parents, not knowing her feller was on a rogue warship at large six thousand miles away.

PO Crawford made his way swiftly aft on the deserted upperdeck to the after mainmast and the ladder leading upwards. The mast had an access hatch halfway up and he navigated his way inside. It was noisy as it carried the exhaust outlet trunkage for both Aft Diesel Generators, one of which was running and fortuitously provided him with much needed warmth. He settled and reopened the hatch and switched on the nightscope. It had 65% battery life and his magazine had eighteen rounds. Where he sat, he had a commanding view of most of the front of the ship.

1210

The zip-lock tie-wraps holding Fowler to a chair in the wardroom were purposefully tight and cutting and he sat slumped forward his wet, sweaty and lank hair flopping forward and dribbles of blood issuing from his nose onto his now-filthy white shirt. His trousers had been removed, and he was also minus a sock. The pasting he took when some of Topsy's mutineers stormed the Captain's cabin was substantial and brutal, and he had a hairline fracture on his collarbone where he'd been bodily manhandled down one deck to the wardroom on Topsy's orders. Now all the Officers were crowded in there, manacled with zip-locks and under armed guard whilst Fowler sat as the accused in the dock for all their crimes.

Topsy took a swig from a freshly opened bottle of vodka he'd liberated from the Wardroom bar, and slung his rifle over his shoulder, moving toward Fowler. He raised his right boot and placed it on the Officer's shoulder, which made him gasp in pain. Fowler raised his head, still a little stunned from the earlier assault.

"Right! Lieutenant Commander fucking Fowler ... Patrick Fowler ... R ... N!" Topsy said, loudly and aggressively. "I'm afraid I have some really fucking grave news for you, matey! Sorry! I mean ... *sir!*"

Fowler looked up at Topsy. "Turner! Release me at once! That is a direct order!" His voice was croaky and gaspy.

Topsy removed his boot and turned to his audience. "Lads! Laaaadsss! Do you think we should let this fucking twat go?"

"Shoot the cunt!" said one.

"Kill him, Tops. Kill him, now!" came another verdict.

Topsy turned back to Fowler, shrugging and grinning. Then he closed-up, really tight to Fowler's haggard face. "Pay attention to me, you snivelling piece of shit. You are responsible for the deaths of about ten of this crew ... "

"... rubbish! You're insane ..." replied Fowler.

"... through your actions ..." Topsy grabbed Fowler's shirt collar hard to straighten him up, "... listen to me, man

… through your actions, we have had to take over this ship, by force."

He released Fowler and turned to the rest of the men again, including the captives.

"The sad thing is, not one of your fucking Officers or Senior Rates had the spine to stand up to you, you cunt! So, they're all as bad as you are, in my book. What do ya say, fellers?"

Fowler struggled against his bonds, fruitlessly. "Turner, let me go, now! That is my final order!" he yelled, his voice almost at a scream. This elicited a "Woooo!" from the mutineers and one of the Able Seamen slid off his seat on the wardroom bar, put his cigarette in the corner of his mouth and crossed the wardroom to where Fowler sat. He very deliberately smacked Fowler around the side of his head and said, "Naughty, fucking naughty!" Fowler struggled more, anger and frustration streaming down his cheeks, as the mutineers cackled scornfully at him. The hysteria was contagious, and the mutineers started on the rest of the prisoners, slapping them and kicking them, playfully. The Ops Officer was sat on the floor and received a hefty kick directly in his balls. He slid sideways gasping and vomited onto the carpet. Fowler's struggles subsided as he realised his bonds are not going to come free. He was a gasping, weeping form. Topsy waved silence from the crowd. They shut up, save for a few giggles.

"Friends!" he said, like a ringmaster. "It is clear what we are to do. The Officers and Senior Rates are all going in the 25-man liferafts!"

The mutineers erupted in more rejoicing. Some were however slightly less pleased and even seemed a bit uneasy.

Fowler raised his head again, saliva and tears making his face shiny. "… and then what? Sail to Tristan de Cuhna and marry one of the local girls? You're no Fletcher-fucking-Christian, Turner! The British Government will have you on every satellite picture in the world. You're an idiot!" Fowler sneered, contemptuously. "A very fucking brave idiot!"

Topsy laughed, somewhat hollowly. "So was Fletcher-fucking-Christian," he said. He then stepped back and perched his backside on the edge of the wardroom table.

"Fowler … we will sit things out. Okay, so there's a lot of trouble when we get back to the UK … big deal, so what, that's life. I reckon we're out of the worst of it now, anyway." He took another long swig of vodka and cleared his throat.

"You authorised the murder of some of your crew. We witnessed it. Your Officers witnessed it, didn't they? You lot are going in the liferafts with the distress beacons going and we will sail away and await the outcome. Hopefully the outcome will be favourable to all concerned … but if they fire on us … or light us up with their radar … well, we'll have to see, won't we?" This was much new news to most of the additional mutineers. The smiles on some faces faded.

"What do you mean?" said Fowler.

Topsy lit a cigarette. "Well … we'll fight back, won't we? We've nothing to lose, you know. 'Course, if they find you first, you'll tell them any old bullshit, won't you?"

"I shall tell them the truth, and nothing else," responded Fowler, somewhat defiantly. "My Officers and Senior Rates will back me up."

Topsy suddenly turned angry. "Yeah, sure thing. You'll tell them anything you want to get you off the hook, won't you, you sad little bastard? You're not bothered who you stitch up, are you? So, it doesn't really matter when they find you, does it? You'll blame us, and twist the story about a bit, and we will be for it, won't we? You won't tell them that you we're making every Junior Rate's life on here a fucking misery, will you? You won't mention the fact that we've been digging out for weeks now with no reward, will you? Topsy paused. "On the *Weymouth* when we dropped the hatches, they promised that everything would be just fucking peachy, and the Skipper and Jimmy would go, and we'd be a happy ship again. But what happened? Fuckers lied to us. Some of us went down, some got kicked outside, but fuck-all changed. It's not gonna be like that, this time. It's gone too far. You've taken it too far, Fowler. So, fuck you!" He rose and dropped the cigarette onto the wardroom carpet, very deliberately crushing it out with his boot.

"We're wasting time, fellers," he said. "Let's fucking get rid of them."

1445

The first 25-man liferaft rolled out of its cradle and fell twenty feet into the cold South Atlantic with a crack against its plastic casing. Instantly a hissing sound came from within, and it broke open revealing a growing orange flower which under gas pressure assistance, formed itself into an octagonal island with a curtained, peaked apex. There it bobbed and was joined by another, then another and two more. Up the starboard waist the Officers, Chiefs and Petty Officers stood now clad in flimsy 'once-only' whole-body coveralls with their General Service lifejackets on, ready to descend the jumping ladder that had been lowered to enable boarding. Topsy's men, now numbering around forty stood round in their foul weather jackets mostly bearing rifles or pistols, most of them not quite knowing what was going on, why they were doing it of even if this was some sort of jape, or exercise. Some others however were more pointed in their actions, jabbing their captives forward with the barrels of their rifles or just pushing them bodily. One or two resisted or made to be awkward to which they were thumped with the stocks of the Self-Loading Rifles. Others from the remaining Junior Ratings cohort stood watching with a mixture of disbelief and fear. Some were already drunk. Topsy stood on the Bridge wing surveying the spectacle whilst three of his trusted Leading Hands supervised two decks below. The armed guards shoved the first prisoners to the gap in the guardrail and men started to disembark their warship into the life rafts below. One Senior Rate, his arm bandaged and strapped, lost his grip on the rope jumping ladder and plunged into the sea. He flailed around as others strove to pick him out of the water and drag him into a raft. Lieutenant Simmo Casey stood at the guardrail and looked up at the Bridge wing where Topsy stood, surveying the operation. "What are you fucking doing?" he yelled. "This is fucking madness! You're going to kill everyone in these liferafts."

Topsy took out his Browning pistol and again fired two shots in the air. Everyone cowered instinctively at the sound of gunshots, even Casey.

"Get in the fucking rafts!" Topsy shouted back at the Officer. "NOW!" and he fired another two rounds, this time at a lower trajectory. The exodus into the rafts continued. John Fisher approached Topsy from behind.

"Topsy! Man … for Christ's sake, eh? Look! This is too much! This is stupid!" he said desperately.

"What is?" said Topsy, calmly.

Fisher rose instantly to the bait. "Aw, come on! This is! Okay, Fowler went a bit too far, but … but God in Heaven, Topsy! You can't do this. Half the ship's company doesn't even know you're doing this. They want it all over and Fowler off the ship in the Falklands. You're tapped in the head, you are, man!"

Topsy lit another cigarette. "Look, Fisher. If you don't dig it, you can always join the bastards in the rafts. You, and anyone else who can't stand the heat. You choose."

"You'll get us all killed!" said Fisher.

"Will I? Then it's better to fucking burn out than to fade away," offered Topsy, anger rising now in his voice. This cunt was standing in his way and needed to get out of it.

Fisher shot back at him, "Dodger's original plan was …"

Topsy reached out and grabbed Fisher's jumper in the chest, pulling him closer. "… well, I don't give a flying fuck about Dodger's 'original plan', because d'you know why? D'you know why, eh, Fisher? Because Dodger's not running the show now. I am! So, if you don't like it, then run along, sweetheart. Get in the rafts with them. Tell any other twat, if they don't want a part of this, then they can go in too. They were all okay sitting about whinging about what was going on, on here … but when it comes to doing summat about it …"

He paused, releasing Fisher and shoving him backward. "Either way, get out of my fucking face, before I fucking slot you."

Fisher stared into Topsy's eyes for just the correct amount of time, turned and walked away, straightening his jumper. Up in the radar compartment on the mainmast, Crawford played the sights of his rifle on Topsy's torso, briefly and then lost him behind some superstructure.

Down on the waist, Able Seaman Richie Foulkes shepherded the Weapons Engineering Officer, Les Tremayne, down the jumping ladder to the life rafts. Tremayne stopped at the top of the ladder.

"Foulkes," he said. "I'm highly disappointed in you. Promising lad like yourself. Letting wankers like this destroy your life."

"Sir," said Foulkes, almost regretfully. "Sir, you're an okay bloke. Most of the pigs … erm … officers are, you know. But the way things have gone … we've got no choice, I suppose …"

"You have a choice, son. Or should I say, you had. There are better ways of resolving this thing, you know …"

Twenty minutes later all the upper and middle management structure of a major UK military asset had been completely disconnected from its foundation and was drifting slowly away from it. On the liferafts immediately an effective plan was being formed and that centred around survival and detection. All the liferafts strung themselves together and Emergency Position Indicating Radio Beacons were deployed, broadcasting a constant 406 MHz signal to overhead satellites of their location. Some wag had rigged a flightdeck hose and hydrant and was dousing the rafts with water spray. The occupants hunkered in and secured the outer covers, instantly carrying out the detailed plans contained in the survival packs.

Topsy witnessed this from the Bridge wing, emotionless. He turned and entered the Bridge through the heavy steel door. Alan Theaker, the navigator's yeoman is close by. The Bridge was full of other spectators and hangers-on. The Leading PTI Roy Sewell was stood close by.

"Clubswinger! Get on the helm. Alan, get me the charts for this end of the world. And find out exactly where we are." Both moved quickly to follow this instruction.

Topsy snatched up the Conning microphone to contact the Machinery Control Room down below. "MCR, Bridge. Have all supplies been remade and engines at two minutes notice?"

"Yes!" came an insolent response who Topsy recognised as Mick Barnes. "About twenty fucking minutes ago."

"And we have all the engines available?"

"Yes," Mick's answer was still salty and insolent. Topsy resolved to maybe later throw the useless, gobby, fat cunt over the side with a concrete lifebuoy sinker tied to his legs.

"Good. Start and select, the port and starboard Tyne engines."

After several attempts, Mick managed to get both engines running and then with some prompting from Ian Rees who'd been summonsed up to help and provide limited expertise, engaged the clutches to drive the two shafts and make the ship move. The only qualified Junior Ratings who could do most of this unaided were now being transferred in their bloodied cocoons of two sleeping bags gaffer taped together to the ship's cold room refrigerator. Control of the engines was eventually passed to the Bridge where LPTI Sewell could control the movement of the ship from a lot better, though that was no guarantee. The amount of expert ship handling, navigation and seamanship skills available was at base-level now. Topsy didn't give a fat fuck. This was his destiny. He would now pay back all the dues he felt he was owed from past grievances with an organisation he felt was corrupt, wrong and flawed.

Through his mattress in his bunk, Dodger felt the characteristic rhythmic pulsing in the structure which gave rise to the feeling the shafts were turning and the ship was moving. Tanzy burst in, fishing something out of his locker. Dodger leaned up on one elbow.

"Whaasapppenin'?" he said.

Tanzy whispered, his voice fearful and a bit desperate, "Topsy's put all the pigs and seniors in the life rafts, Dodger! Fuckin' ell! What the fuck are we gonna do?"

"I dunno, mate. Fuckin' die I suppose! Who's on watch in the MCR?"

"Colin Parsons. Oh, and Mick Barnes. Colin's teaching him all the watchkeeping stuff. Ian's up there too." Tanzy shook his head and smiled grimly.

"That should be a scream. Colin knows fuck all. Mick's as thick as a whale's foreskin and Ian failed his ticket twice."

Dodger swung out of bed and walked through into the mess square, where an enormous stack of beer crates was assembled, the power drinkers already playing uckers and hoovering it down. By the bar, two of them were trying to make a stolen beer pump work. No one even addressed or acknowledged Dodger, so he turned and left.

Chapter Seventeen

Monday 3rd October 1988
East Cove Naval Facility
2235

HMS Athene's Duty Watch were busy preparing her to sail at very short notice. Her Marine Engineers below moved swiftly to raise steam from cold, itself usually a six-hour task now compressed into three since a 'FLASH' signal was received by the Duty Officer of the Day earlier. Since then, the young but pretty switched on Lieutenant reached out via a network of telephone contacts to summons those ashore up at Mount Pleasant Airfield and a few over in Port Stanley to hastily recall them and assemble a credible sailing watch from those available on board. The Captain and a few senior staffers appeared pretty quickly from what they were doing. Right now, the skipper was on a secure, encrypted direct line with Fleet Operations Officer in Northwood, having spoken to a Ministry of Defence intelligence specialist in Whitehall. The

First Lieutenant had yet to appear, so *Athene's* own Operations Officer occupied himself with numbers returning and their fit state to man harbour stations and three of their ship staff who were on a Rest and Recuperation expedition on Volunteer Point, prodding penguins and fur seals.

One man, in warmly wrapped in civilian clothing scampered up the gangway, a bit dishevelled. The Quartermaster, dressed in DPM camouflage gear, met him at the top of the gangway and greeted him warmly, "Just made it, Brian. You were lucky. There's still about twenty ashore."

"Yeah. There all at the hockey match piss-up. The bus has broke down." Brian pegged himself in.

"Well, it's a bit late for them. We're sailing, ASAP," said the QM.

"Why, what the fuck's up?"

The QM shrugged. "Oh, apparently there's an Argie sub in the patrol zone. Skipper wants it out of the way now so we can do the handover to *Warwick* quickly and fuck off home for Christmas."

Brian wasn't entirely convinced. "Really? Roll on the *Warwick* getting here. I'm fucking pissed off with this."

"Yeah, me too mate. Me too," said the QM, as he watched Brian stumble away.

Tuesday 4th October 1988
0912

Topsy and Alan Theaker had *Warwick* on a course heading on bearing 125 magnetic to take the ship, now doing twelve knots, somewhere over the top of South Georgia, roughly 800 miles east of the Falkland Islands. Topsy knew from his job in the ships Operations Room that this didn't preclude it being reached by the Tornadoes based at Mount Pleasant Airfield but his judgement, agreed by his close cohort of confidents who were now reducing in numbers alarmingly, the UK Government wouldn't attack *Warwick* anyway. He made himself believe they were in a position of strength to negotiate and conveyed this to his collective. Right now, he stood on the Bridge studying the expansive chart covering the Southern Ocean down to the towering splendour of South Georgia. If things got really bad maybe he could anchor in one of the harbours on the island and sweat it out. Yeah, that was an idea. He had no idea about endurance, weather reports or other such mission affective issues. All he was bothered about was he'd got rid of those cunts and now he had the ship.

Dodger appeared on the Bridge and Topsy looked sideways, regarding him contemptuously.

"What the fuck do you want?" he said, suspiciously.

"What's going on, Topsy?" asked Dodger.

Topsy returned his gaze to the chart, not really looking at anything in particular. "We're just steaming up the Solent. We should be in Portsmouth in about five minutes. Wanker."

LPTI Sewell chortled at the helm. Topsy continued, "If you really want to know, Dodger, we're steaming on a South Easterly course at twelve knots, to get away from the life rafts."

"Why?" said Dodger, stepping further onto the Bridge.

"So that we can get to … here." He brought his finger down on an area of white, north of a landmass Dodger recognised as the distinct shape of South Georgia.

Dodger regarded this and then looked back at Topsy. "Why?" he asked, once again, with the same voice.

"We wait …"

"For what?"

"To negotiate …"

"Negotiate what?"

Topsy rolled his eyes, irritated. "To work out when they can have their ship back."

Dodger shook his head and smiled weakly. "And then …?"

Topsy then sighed, exasperated, adolescently. "We all go home, Dodger. I get nicked, along with you … and half the ship's company, and we all go down. Don't bother me … I've done time before; it's a piece of piss. Anyway, I'll make my own fortune with my story in the papers, even if some dickhead wants to write a book about it. I'm sorted. I don't fucking care, Dodger. Is that good enough for you?"

The Bridge fell silent. Everyone moved their gaze elsewhere than this conversation. Topsy returned his attention to the chart, leaning forward a little.

"Topsy … have you told the rest of the lads about all this?" said Dodger, trying to retain calm in his manner.

"Not yet." He paused and then paused some more. "But I will …"

Dodger had Topsy on the hook, and about five or six people were hearing this. "When?"

Topsy turned and raised his binoculars, looking out to sea from the starboard Bridge window. "When I'm fucking ready," he said, lowering the binoculars. "Anything else?"

"Yes. What happens when they sent half the fleet to look for us?"

"Depends …"

"On what?"

Topsy had reached almost the end of his rope now. In his mind, he wanted to pull out his pistol and shoot Dodger straight in the face but feared that may hamper his ambitions a bit.

"Look. If they come looking for us and give us grief, which I hope they don't, but if they do Dodger, we will take them on. We've got enough to go to action, if needed. If they come peacefully and give us a few guarantees … then I'll be happy."

"Guarantees?" said Dodger. "Like what?"

"None of your fucking business. You're not running the show, now. You fucked it up." He returned to scanning the horizon with his binoculars. Dodger stood still, his eyes burning into Topsy's head. After ten seconds, Topsy slowly lowered the binoculars again and looked directly at Dodger. "You still here?" he said.

1102

Fifteen hundred metres astern of *Warwick* and in perfect synchrony with her speed a periscope broke the surface of the grey sea. Several metres below this and well hidden from sight, the Soviet Kilo-Class submarine *Vologda* tracked *Warwick* diligently. A KGB contact in the Ministry of Defence Main Building in Whitehall had picked up the blitz of messages now moving between Government Departments and before long, the Soviet Navy had an asset on the rogue destroyer's tail. After a minute, the periscope retracted, and the submarine changed its position to observe another angle.

A hundred and thirty miles west of this, the six life rafts jostled together in a worsening sea. Many of the occupants were cold, miserable and feeling the effects of the merciless, chilly ocean right under their backsides. Fowler sat emotionless amongst them, his eyes shut and his face pulsing still from the blows issued by Topsy and his gang. He had managed to sneak some Valium and Codeine out with him when he went to get changed and had a couple inside his bloodstream, which at least took away some of the pain in his collarbone.

Above their heads, the EPIRB had quickly done its job.

Captain Desmond Slack appeared on the Bridge of *RFA White Rover* with a handful of papers and his tie loosened at the neck. He looked knackered. "Officer of the Watch, I have the ship," he said.

"You have the ship," replied the OOW.

Slack looked out of the window at the choppy waters. "QM, starboard fifteen. Set revolutions one, eight zero. Officer of the Watch, get me the Engineer. Steer course zero-five-zero."

"Steer course, zero-five-zero. Aye sir," responded the Quartermaster.

The Executive Officer arrived, buttoning up his shirt. "Sir. What's the problem?" he said.

"We're heading out to an EPIRB distress signal, coming from one of our life rafts," replied Slack seriously and grimly.

Latham and Slack's eyes locked together. "*Warwick?*"

"Yeah. Seems so." Both Officers looked worried. Very worried.

"Course to steer, zero-five-zero, sir. Revolutions one eight zero, passed and repeated, sir. Ship's speed, ten knots," interrupted the Quartermaster.

"Very good," said Slack, still looking at Latham.

"Are they in trouble?" said Latham.

"Yes. But not in the 'sinking type'," replied Slack. The Quartermaster looked round.

Latham thought for a bit and then reduced his voice to a whisper. "You don't mean …"

Slack also lowered his voice, turning his head away from those others present on *White Rover's* Bridge. "… could be. *Athene's* just put to sea from East Cove and …" he looked down at the document in his hand, "… is proceeding with despatch to somewhere just Northeast of South Georgia."

"South Georgia? That's miles from where we were supposed to rendezvous with *Warwick*." For Latham, one of the RFAs rising stars it was quickly dropping into place. "This explains it all."

"Indeed." Slack went back to the chart table, Latham following him. When he got there, he said, "You'd better alert the doc. We may be picking up survivors. Apparently, HQ Northwood are planning to get the Special Boat Service down at some time very soon."

Latham's face dropped further. "Shit!"

Two hundred miles astern, *HMS Athene* came up to full speed heading out past Cape Pembroke on her port side into the South Atlantic. The frigate had been on station for five and a half months, and looked purposeful and battered, it's funnel pluming heat as its Babcock and Wilcox boilers roared down below, and the ship's company sobered up and tried to come to terms with some-or-some-or-another new task. Out on her flightdeck, the ship's Westland Lynx helicopter was being ranged on deck, her blades recently unfolded and locked and the ship's flight going through meticulous checks in the fading light. Soon it would be airborne to pick up the errant hikers from Volunteer Point to complete her itinerary of staff.

On her Bridge, the Captain appeared, exchanged detail about navigation and status of the ship from various members of his staff and then went to the back of the Bridge, picking up the main broadcast microphone.

"D'yer'hearthere! Captain speaking," he said. "Many rumours have permeated the ship in the past few hours relating to the nature of our swift departure from East Cove. Well, now we are at sea, and away from prying eyes, I can reliably inform you all that the latest rumour, that of our relief ship, *HMS Warwick* having difficulties was partially true. What was not true, however, was that she is sinking. There seems to have been some crew problems on board, and we are heading at full speed to ensure the *Warwick* has safe passage to the Falklands. We are just under two days sailing from her and will go into Defence Watches from midnight, tonight. We may come up against some token resistance and may have to board *Warwick* at some time to restore control and arrest those concerned with the problem. That is all."

Elsewhere in *Athene,* sailors looked at each other with huge apprehension and confusion.

Mount Pleasant Airfield, Falkland Islands
1416

The C130K Hercules XV204 reached the entry of runway 23 and rolled to a stop. After a quick contact with the control tower, all four Allison turboprops ramped up and the aircraft instantly moved forward, gaining speed and lifting off in an impressively short space of time and distance for such a seemingly bulky and cumbersome airframe. It banked instantly left whilst still climbing and getting on course eastward out toward its target.

The Flight Engineer, Sargeant Freddie Topham stood behind the Pilot, Flight Lieutenant Lionel Pearson and First Officer and Co-Pilot Warrant Officer 'Bungy' Edwards. The plane butted through the turbulence put up by the scudding grey mizzle, then cleared the low 'muck' into a clear, brighter vista of billowing white clouds and harsh sunshine overhead. All three donned aviator-style sunglasses.

"How long have we got over the target area?" asked Topham into his headset microphone. He'd been bumped onto this classified mission at the last minute as the 1312

Squadron's Duty Flight Engineer was currently ill with the shits.

Pearson turned in his seat. "Sixteen minutes!" he yelled.

"Right," said Topham. "If we do this right, we're on the SBS run, aren't we?"

"Yeah!" replied the First Officer. "If, and when the lazy, fat bastards arrive. Looks like It'll be all over by then, though."

XV204 levelled out at 20000. The calculation was with full tanks, the aircraft was right on the end of its range. The other C130K equipped to refuel the air contingent was currently grounded with a flight controls defect so they were on instruction to get there by direct line, circle and take some pictures and get back. One problem was they were currently awaiting American satellite updates on *Warwick's* position. The Spanish submarine had detached once the uplink brief had been sent and was heading home, low on fuel and power herself, so at that particular time, no one knew where the Type 42 Destroyer actually was. Pearson was sure on one thing; he had no fuel to go looking for the ship and his fitted radar was practically no use to find surface targets at range. He just hoped Headquarters would come up with something in the next two hours because if *Warwick* had changed course, he was heading into empty ocean.

Chapter Eighteen

Wednesday 5th October 1988
2M Port Junior Rating's Bathroom
0745

Dodger entered the bathroom, allowing the ship's motion to swing the door shut behind him with a bang. Topsy was the only other person in there, topless with his Number Eight uniform work trousers on looking muscular and menacing, his blonde hair was carefully coiffured into his characteristic Teddy-Boy 'DA' style with heavy applications of Brylcreem. He gooshed shaving cream into his hand and paused briefly to look somewhat contemptuously at Dodger who at first avoided his brown-eyed gaze. Dodger went to a sink next-door-but-one to Topsy and dumped his dhoby-bag on the sill behind the taps, putting in the plug and pressing the taps equally to fill the stainless-steel sink.

"Tops," he said, carefully.

"Yep …" said Topsy. He applied the cream and dunked his razor, tapping the hot water off loudly. He continued to shave, loud, manly rasps interrupted by dunks and taps. Dodger washed his face quietly.

"You back in it with us, then?" said Topsy.

Dodger stopped washing, still looking downwards at the water. "In what?" he said.

"The mutiny. The whole thing. You were the cause of it all, pal." Topsy resumed rasping away at his beard on his neck, pulling his chin up for purchase on the razor.

Dodger stood straight and turned toward his companion. "Hold on, just a fucking minute! All I wanted was Fowler off the ship. You went and put the bastards in the life rafts! You've sent them to their fucking deaths. They won't fucking survive this."

Topsy continued shaving, "Dodger, you're in on it. Like it or not. You're in on it."

Dodger was incensed and frightened in equal parts. "Fuckin' well not! Count me out!"

Topsy gave two brisk swoops of the razor and dropped it into the sink. Then he flashed out an arm, sideways and made connection with Dodger's hair. With a frightening amount of strength, he twisted Dodger around and downwards, so he was suddenly facing the ceiling, with his neck in contact with the sink. Topsy held Dodger there and calmly, malevolently stepped astride Dodger's flailing body, reaching inside his own toiletries bag pulling out a Stanley knife and with his thumb, opened out the blade. He then pressed the blade into Dodger's cheek, just below the eye, breaking the skin. Dodger's face was a mask of terror. Topsy closed his face toward Dodger's and lowered his voice almost to whisper. "Listen! Can you hear it? Can you?" He started to grin. "I can hear it, Dodger. I can, you know. I can hear ... *fear!* Now, all I want from the likes of you and a few other of the knobheads on this ship is a little co-operation. Maybe we can come out of this with a little dignity." Topsy paused and stopped grinning, his face now almost serious. "You do understand 'dignity', do you, Dodger? Do you?"

Dodger nodded his head, microscopically, his eyes as wide as they could get. Topsy released his grip on Dodger's hair and straightened up but kept him pinned to the sink just by the point of the blade, which had now gone through the skin and tissue on his face and was in direct contact with his cheekbone. Dodger could feel it, scraping as Topsy's weight shifted with the movement of the ship. A rivulet of blood trickled backwards towards his ear.

"If you cross me, Dodger, I shall fuck you up. Believe me," Topsy said, with determination. He then withdrew the Stanley Knife blade and threw the device in his dhoby-bag, stepped off Dodger's prone form and left him inverted, perched by his neck on the cold steel of the sink.

British Forces Falkland Islands Headquarters, Mount Pleasant Airfield

1306

Almost at the intersection of the Port Stanley to Darwin and Mount Pleasant to Mare Harbour roads, over the scarp of a bracken covered hill opposite an aptly named piece of water called Macho Pond just south of the airfield, the Commanding Officer of all UK Armed Forces on the Falklands has his Headquarters. It's an unassuming spectacle, drive past it and you'd miss it, resembling a hospital or a posh hotel set into the lee of the hill. Inside, the adjacent Briefing Room to the Commanding Officer's outer office was manned by eight people, three civilian defence analysts and four Senior staffers, and the Officer Commanding, Brigadier Mike Jones MBE of the Royal Logistic Corps himself. One of his Staff Officers was Commander Phil Chapman, in the role of Senior Naval Officer, Falkland Islands and it was he who was leading the brief, having just finished a secure telephone conversation with Naval HQ at Northwood back in the UK. This call had been intercepted and decoded by Russian Agents on an intelligence gathering vessel parked 60 miles off the island of St Helena, so it was less secure than was believed.

On a portable whiteboard, eight unremarkably dark, low-resolution images are being displayed.

"Is that it?" said Jones, disappointed, obviously expecting detail and clarity. The RAF Staff Officer stared straight ahead.

"'Afraid so, sir," replied Chapman. "The night-vision shots aren't much better. There's very little happening. Be better if we got day shots, then we can ascertain what their state of readiness is." Chapman seemed to be getting some purchase on the RAF staffer in front of his boss. This competition was endemic between the two uniforms.

"What's the risk?" asked Jones, tersely. He looked at everyone, because they'd mostly been a bit quiet, and he needed some way ahead on this. Back home, the nation was waking up to the news that one of their warships was rogue and it was in his back yard with Christ-knows-who in charge of the pretty-well armed thing. He had zero idea what a Type 42 Destroyer was or could do mind you, let alone what the greater situation was or its cause and effect. All he wanted was it fixed. Right now. These lot in front of him needed to come up with some options, pretty damned quick.

"Mmmm. Minimal at the moment, I'd say, sir. It's doubtful they won't know how to properly operate the long-range Seadart anti-air missile system and the safe keys for that are out of their reach," said Chapman.

"And ..." said Jones.

"Maybe not the Vulcan Phalanx either ... the Close In Weapon System ... but we can't be sure. Their air-search radar seems to be switched off all the time. We could literally overfly them, and they wouldn't notice."

"You sure?"

"Well, we do need intelligence. And we need to know their resolve." Chapman let that hang in the air, because it was true. They had nothing yet about what was happening. *White Rover* was closing on the life-rafts and the ship was dark on all channels of communications.

Jones stood up, suddenly and adjusted his belt. "Right. I'll clear it with the big man and Northwood. We'll do it today." He pointed at the pictures on the white board. "We need better material than this. Besides, the SBS are taking their time to get ready and get down here.

"When are they due?" said one of the analysts.

"Tomorrow. Maybe the day after," said Colonel 'Sandy' Bennett, the Army's chief Staff Officer. "*Warwick* could be out of range by then. We'd have to stop the frigate to drop them onto her. None of the Boat Squadron coming are air trained so can't parachute and our SAS assets are busy in the Gulf, right now. It all gets very messy." Jones looked at the RAF staffer. "Let me know your availability by 1400. I need that Fat Albert over that ship before the light fades."

Port Waist – P2 Gun Mount

1645

Leading Seaman 'Jock' McLelland pulled his snood up round his face after taking a large gobful of Foster's lager from the tin in his gloved hand. He tossed the empty can over into the southern Atlantic Ocean and reaches down into the box at the base of the General Purpose Machine Gun's plinth both he and his trusty young assistant Able Seaman 'Pansy' Potter are manning. Jock fitted a lot of poor stereotypes: he was considered a naval relic in Topsy's messdeck and a bit of a joke, being about twenty years past his expected promotion to Petty Officer and, at 43, was much of an oddity amongst younger men around him being born just after World War II. For that matter, the weatherblown, veiny face, the croaky voice from smoking a million fags and the sardonic, cynical, fast-outdated attitude set him in aspic and made him the anti-hero amongst a few, and a figure of scorn for others. Pansy had the misfortune to share a Part of Ship with him in employment and manning this machine gun at Action Stations. Everywhere Jock went, a miasma of alcohol fumes followed him, and this held him and his career in a vice-like grip, anchoring him into this sad, decrepit and pitiful character.

He fished out two tins, issuing a 'tsssst' to Pansy who turned and caught the one Jock threw him. Pansy looked ill and smiled at Jock submissively. Then he leaned forward and puked copiously on the rough, grey deck.

"Ho there boy!" exclaimed Jock, laughing. "Straight out o' there! Divnae hang on tae it, eh? Oot ya basta!" Jock opened and swigged again. Pansy straightened up. This 'drinking a lot of lager' wasn't his game at all.

"Jock," he said, wearily, his nose streaming and flecks of vomit on his face and chin. "Let's get this th … thing going. Then we can piss off to bed. I'm fuckin' freezing!"

Jock deftly loaded the machine gun like a consummate, sober expert. "There, y'see? Nae bother!" and he backed toward the hangar and picked up the wired comms headset. "PDC, P4. Testing Comms, how do you hear me?"

Down in the Operations Room the Point Defence Co-ordinator, or more correctly a Leading Hand who'd volunteered to do the job and hadn't much of a clue, responded in his microphone. "Loud and clear, Jock. How me?"

Jock belched into the mic. "Loud and clear al-also."

"Jock," said the PDC operator. "You still pissed?" There was concern in his voice.

Jock was slightly irked by this. "What me? Get straight tae fuck, will ya?" Pansy vomited again. Jock then lost his cool a bit. "Aw, fae fuck's sake, Pansy! Yer wasting beer! Jeezis!"

Pansy wiped his mouth on his sleeve. "Sorry matey," he said, mustering a weak grin.

Twenty-two miles away in XV204, Squadron Leader Steve Sawbury made final positional checks and dropped the aircraft in increments until they were two hundred feet above the swirling white tops, feeling the turbulence whipped up by the ocean. His First Officer this time was Flt Lt Lionel Pearson with Sgt Freddie Topham in the back as Engineer. Further back in the hold sat a Staff Sargeant and Captain from the Royal Corps of Signals and an intelligence civilian civil servant from General Command Headquarters. He'd puked several times into a fairly full sick bag and wasn't taking this buffeting well either. The Seargent unzipped his holdall and took out a Nikon SLR Camera and attached a long-range zoom lens to it. Up in the cockpit, the First Officer switched on the navigation radar.

On *Warwick*, Able Seaman Foulkes's electronic countermeasures panel instantly blipped. The UAA1 array at the top of the mast near where Petty Officer Crawford was holed up received two sweeps from XV204s navigation radar.

"Fucking hell!" said Foulkes.

A freshly liberated shipment of crisps and biscuits had appeared in the Stoker's mess square and were being demolished. Suddenly the Main Broadcast alarm sounded, which to any matelot nailed you dead as soon as you hear it. Topsy's voice followed it, booming and with authority. "Hands to action stations! Hands to action stations! Assume Damage Control State 1, Condition Zulu!"

Dodger rolled out of his bed quickly, in his pants and socks. He reached for his overalls and donned them, grabbing his boots from the boot rack. He proceeded out of the bunk space past flailing bodies and tired and pissed men, all staggering a bit uselessly. He put the strap of his respirator over his shoulder and undid the top flap, fishing out his anti-flash hood and gloves. As he went up the ladder, he donned these automatically. He passed Jumper Crossley in the passageway in a towel and flip flops, having just returned from the shower.

"Jumper! Get your arse into gear and get down the After Engine Room, will you?"

Jumper flicked a forehead finger salute at his Action Stations Leading Hand. "Roger, shippers!" he said, with unnerving cheery mirth. Dodger was unimpressed at this, considering Jumper had killed Harry Wilmot not long ago and possibly had his knife in his dhoby bag. He journeyed up the starboard passageway forward and reached the Aft Engine Room door which led downwards to his Action Station and drew a deep breath, trying to suppress the gathering fear and dread he'd held in his heart for over six years.

Sawbury dropped the C130 to eighty feet and Topham pointed out a misty shape up ahead. It was a warship. Thank fuck the intel had been right. The ship was presenting its port quarter to his aircraft which meant the bridge couldn't see his approach, which was good. "Open the ramp," he instructed

Topham. Who flipped the switch and disappeared into the cargo bay to ready the Signals people to get onto it with their camera. Sawbury edged the nose to starboard so he could fly up the port side of *Warwick*, open out, circle around and fly down the starboard side. Hopefully the Signals people would get all the imagery they needed, and he could fuck off because fuel would be tight, once again and he was flying straight into a steely westerly on his way back to the Falklands.

On the Bridge of *Warwick* everyone closed up in overalls and anti-flash hoods and gloves, Topsy the only one with his headgear pulled back. The Hercules boomed past the port side, low, fast, close and very loud, startling everyone in there. Topsy watched it open out and bank, catching a glimpse of camouflaged individuals stood on its tail ramp.

Alan Theaker approached Topsy. "I bet there's Boat Service fuckers on that Albert," he said.

Topsy nodded, his eyes ablaze. He rushed over to the other side of the Bridge and raised his binoculars to look at the aircraft, briefly. Dropping the binoculars, he turned to the communications rating and said, "Stan! Get out on any channel. Tell them to back the fuck off or we'll start shooting."

Stan, a young Radio Operator, looked terrified. "I can't do that, Topsy! For fucks sake!"

Topsy yelled, "Just fucking do it! If you don't this ship will be teeming with nasty bastards with balaclavas who will kick all our fucking heads in!"

Stan pressed the handset to broadcast on Channel 16, "RAF Hercules! This is warship *Warwick*. You are warned not to approach the ship. We will fire on your bearing if you do."

The Hercules swung round in front of *Warwick*, dropped low and lined up to pass down the starboard side. Sawbury had done this a couple of times in the past with Russian and Argentine ships, just to piss them off and scare them shitless. He banked the starboard wing upward to show the ship it's underside and maximise the effect. The plane passed just over thirty feet from nearest contact with any of *Warwick's* structure, but everyone on the Bridge instinctively ducked. As it passed the stern, Pansy Potter on S4 released a volley of 7.62mm rounds from his GPMG into the underside of the plane. His mentor was still sleeping off his latest session down in 3P messdeck, and Pansy was hungover, still drunk and shitting himself.

Three of the rounds ricocheted inside the cargo bay and ten hit the fuselage, puncturing the thin skin. Sawbury saw the tracers arcing up and quickly manoeuvred the aircraft to avoid further impacts, almost spilling people off the ramp area. The other gunners arrayed along the starboard side saw the firing as some kind of cue and opened up their batteries too but the aircraft became quickly out of their range. As he banked the aircraft slightly and levelled off, Sawbury witnessed multiple guns firing and fearing the Vulcan Phalanx opening up and swiftly bringing his slow aeroplane crashing down

He gave the First Officer a cut-throat sign to signify the end of the mission. "Let's get the fuck out of here! Fucking mad bastards!" he said.

The aircraft climbed to a thousand feet and levelled off and they then overflew a dark shape beneath the water, which the intelligence operative pointed out to the photographer. He in turn fired off several pictures of the submarine. "That's Russian! Kilo class! Jesus wept!" he said.

Half an hour later, Topsy and some of his lieutenants had both Jock McLelland and Pansy Potter mustered by their machine gun on the upper deck, He was furious.

"You stupid, piss-ignorant, Jock twat! We are right in the shit, now! We might as well have shot the fucking Queen! What chance have we got now of getting out of this in one piece, eh?"

Jock stared at the deck. He stunk of stale booze. Pansy was similarly subdued. "Soz Tops," said Jock lowly.

"You fucking-well will be, too! Get the fuck out of my sight before I fucking waste you, you useless piece of shit. And take your fucking bum-chum with you." Jock and Pansy scampered away. Topsy turns to his men.

"Alan. Get the ship east. Somewhere over the top of South Georgia. Tell the lads that Albert had SAS or SBS or something on it. That's why we shot at it." Alan looked furtive and puzzled, but unlikely to counter Topsy's way ahead. "Okay. Tops, have the Stokers been in touch?"

"Nope. What's the problem?"

"Oh … er, the water-making gear's knackered," said Alan. "We've only got fifteen tons of fresh water. So, they've locked the showers. And there's more good news. We've only got two days of fuel left … if that."

"Fuck!" said Topsy under his breath. "Okay, I'll talk to them." He walked over to the guardrail and stared out to sea. He lit a cigarette, pondering what next.

Chapter Nineteen

Thursday 6th October 1988
44°34'45" S 42°42'46" W
0555

Most of the five life-rafts' occupants were dozing. They'd been apart from *Warwick* now for over 24 hours and had fortunately drifted against the prevailing wind and with the sea current westward by about sixty miles since they boarded their uneasy rides. Water had been issued from the on-board survival packs, but no one had eaten as was the standard practice and observed official guidance. Lt Cdr Les Tremayne, *HMS Warwick's* now ex-Weapons Engineer Officer was taking his shift with his head out of the waterproof flap scanning the horizon for activities. The morning was bright, and the glare of the sun glinted uncomfortably off the individual wavelets into Tremayne's eyes. In the very far distance at about 35000 feet, he could see a commercial airliner crayoning the turquoise sky. His lips were glazed with salt and his skin felt a bit raw against the biting wind.

As the connected knot of life-rafts turned lazily in the sea, his lookout port brought him facing southwest. There, on the horizon was the unmistakable shape of a ship, bows-on, coming at them.

"Hey!" he yelled. "It's a ship! It's a ship!"

More people rose to struggle for a view and Smith-Howlett let off a distress flare. The ship, rapidly approaching, replied with both her siren and her floodlights. This broke out a spontaneous cheer from the rafters. Fowler sat back in the raft glowering, head down. "Bastards," he said, bitterly and resentfully. Whether it was addressed to the Royal Fleet Auxiliary, his relieved raftmates or the mutinous crew back on *Warwick* was firmly inside his head.

The ship came about, beam on to shield the rafts with many of her ship staff huddled at the guardrails, and a rescue boat launched. The rafts were emptied, and the survivors taken aboard dishevelled but grateful and the crew of *RFA White Rover* took good care of them, silently ushering them below, revered in respect and slightly in awe.

Captain's Cabin, *RFA White Rover*
0935

Fowler emerged from Slack's personal bathroom in his very palatial cabin, towelling his hair and wearing Slack's own bathrobe. Slack poured freshly brewed coffee and placed the cup next to a full English Breakfast on his table he'd got the head chef to quickly knock up. Elsewhere, *White Rover*'s crew were busy getting the rest of Fowler's surviving crew of Officers and Senior Ratings similarly seen to and fed and fortunately a stash of wire-framed camp beds had appeared with spare military sleeping bags they'd embarked years ago as a Disaster Relief package. Of the one hundred and one rescued, only three needed triage medical care for the effects of exposure and the sea and injuries but all had a once over by *White Rover*'s Medical Officer just to check their overall health.

Fowler sat at the table and declined Slack's offer of milk, sipping his beverage and still towelling his hair. His face and torso were a mass of bruises from the roughing up at the hands of Topsy and his men, and his collarbone stabbed pain and looked bruised, but he showed no heed to this.

"The doc will be up in an hour or so," said Slack. "He's dealing with the worst of the cases, first. I've got the stewards to cobble some breakfast together for you."

"No thank you. I'm not hungry," said Fowler, humourlessly and curtly.

Slack was somewhat astonished. "Surely …" he began.

Fowler shook his head. He rose and went to Slack's cabinet helped himself to a Scotch. "You don't mind, do you?" he said, almost demanding Slack didn't mind at all.

"No, not at all. Fill your boots, please." Slack was genial and giving. His crew loved him. He watched Fowler take moderate gulps of the whiskey. Fowler topped up the glass and rejoined him by his writing desk.

"So," Slack said. "What the fuck happened?"

"I'll save it for the inquiry, if you don't mind, shipmate," said Fowler, his voice roughened up by the Scotch.

"Courts Martial all round?"

"Oh yes. I should fuckin' coco," Fowler offered, sipping the Scotch again. He leaned forward. "In fact, the only person who will come out of this relatively unscathed will be me. I'm going to make it my mission to see that all of those … bastards suffer for this."

"Pardon?" Slack was taken aback. Who did he mean, exactly?

"They're all going down, one way or another." Fowler locked Slack's gaze, meaningfully.

"Who?" said Slack. "What do you mean?"

Fowler suddenly broke out of his thought plan. He stood up, downing the contents of the glass in one. "I really need to get a message to the Commanding Officer, British Forces on the Falklands," he said. "It is rather urgent, you know."

"Tell me. I will see to it straight away."

Fowler pointed, "Okay. Now listen. The mutineers have made it very plain that they have no intention of giving the ship back. They said they would have no hesitation of engaging opposing forces if needed. You are lucky that you found us, before they found you."

"What?" Slack was baffled by this.

"I'm telling you, man, they are set on nothing more than trouble. I don't think we'll be seeing *Warwick* again. In my honest opinion, their only option is to defect. Okay, some of the married ones and a few others will want to come home. They'll face some … minor charge. But the hard-core mutineers have precious little to lose, now. They can't cruise around forever, and by my reckoning they'll be out of fuel by late tomorrow at the latest. So, it's a good job you found us, so we can warn Whitehall of their intentions." Fowler paused, as if to consider what he'd just said, because although it sounded fanciful, to him it also sounded factual. "Have you got a satellite fix on *Warwick*?"

"Sure. She's about two hundred miles north, northeast of South Georgia. They're doing seven knots, course 135. There's a Yank satellite right over her now."

"Right," said Fowler, feeling vindicated. "See, they're not that stupid, are they? Staying out of reach of aircraft … no fuckin' dummies, that lot, are they?"

"Well, actually a Hercules buzzed them yesterday, and they received small arms fire as they passed," said Slack. He wasn't going to tell Fowler this just yet, but it seemed pertinent.

"And … they bring it down?"

"No. A couple of hits but the aircraft made it back with a few Jimpy holes in it." Slack went further. "But by the looks of it, your defection story holds water."

Fowler paused again. This was groundbreaking. "Why?" he said.

"On the way out from the ship, the Albert's crew photographed what looks to be a Soviet Kilo-Class submarine on station near the ship. It was at periscope depth, about six miles from Warwick." Slack rose, loosening his tie. "We'll have to let *Athene* know."

"What's *Athene* doing? Back at East Cove, still?"

"Christ, no, man! She's on her way out to *Warwick*. They think it's a minor case of naughty crew syndrome and readying themselves to board. If the *Kilo* gets snarled up in this it could sink both ships, very easily. My God!"

1430

About thirty members of *Warwick*'s Junior Rate cohort stood on the quarterdeck in various states of dress, however wrapped up as the South Atlantic bounded its main literally feet from them. Occasionally a 'goffer' – naval parlance for decent-sized wave – would crash against the ship's side and break into the space beneath the flightdeck, showering them with spray which was cold and felt like danger. Stood on the second rung of the ladder upwards to it was Leading Stores

Accountant John Fisher and by the side of him lay eight bodies, wrapped tightly in their sleeping bag and gaffer tape shrouds. Three of the attended had volunteered the grim task of cocooning the remaining dead men, one of them Tanzy Lee, who was physically sick when he saw Harry Wilmot's cold grey visage and then puked more when it came to wrap Doc Savage, his head empty of brains, a manic eyeball dangling by its optic nerve and the lower jaw half smiling yellowed teeth. Someone found his treasured knife and that was taped to his body. Now they lay on the wet deck like fat pupae. Dead, sad, fat pupae.

"Gents," said John Fisher, solemnly. "Thanks for getting your arses out of bed and coming down to pay tribute to your shipmates." He clung onto the handrails of the ladder as the ship took another lurch. "We've lost eight decent souls in the past few days, and we needn't have. One Officer's actions and the kickback to that has resulted in a situation we all never thought we'd be in. It's a bit like what happened in '82 in Corporate, in fact when we lost eighty-odd matelots because of stupidity and madness. Control and reasoning were lost as soon as the first firing began." He paused and drew a breath. "So here we are."

Fisher paused again. His emotions and anger were sweeping through his very person. Everyone else stood in silence with the ocean whooshing about them.

"LMEM Wilmott, Leading Chef Savage, LWEM Cookson, Able Seaman Sowerby, Able Seaman Prentiss, Able Seaman Bradley, WEM Drysdale and Steward Wakefield all died following an illegal movement to take control of this ship from the Command structure it already had in place. I am also told that some of us ... yes, us ... kicked a Petty Officer to death in his messdeck and then dumped his body over the fucking side. Never mind the causes ... these ..." Fisher pointed down at the bags, "... these are the fucking results." Fisher then noticed Dodger stood near the back in the shadows and felt his anger rise further. "Had we all not followed mob rule and instinct, these lot would still be with us."

Fisher looked down at a piece of paper, he'd scribbled notes upon. "If you've come here to pay respect, then fucking-well pay respect. If you've come to feel guilty then I have no fucking sympathy for you. Their lives are on you and anyone else who dies on this fucking ship from now on. Let's have a minute of silence to think about our lost brothers ..."

All attending bowed their heads for sixty long, miserable, sea-sprayed seconds. When it was over, Fisher called out. "Okay. Let's get round them and commit them to the deep. Respectfully and with dignity. Ship's company … ho!"

Every person came sharply to attention. Fisher led the way, at first stooping and struggling alone with Doc's slippery, heavy corpse until two, three, five, ten … everyone joined in to lift their fallen comrades at shoulder height and gently pitch them over the guardrails of the quarterdeck into the thronging wake behind the ship. The bodies were each weighted with an assortment of 10kg and 20kg barbell plates nicked from LPT Sewell's own weight-training collection and they quickly rolled over in the foam and were gone into the depths of the ocean and downwards to their resting place. Fisher saluted and everyone followed his lead until he witnessed the last corpse vanish from view then snapped his hand down to his side, tears rolling down his and many other's cheeks.

He turned to the men around him. "Dismiss," he said lowly, but no one seemed eager to depart. Eventually in ones, twos and threes they all left by the door at the front of the quarterdeck back into the warmth of 2 deck. Only Dodger remained and when he was sure everyone was gone, he approached John Fisher.

"Moving stuff," he said.

"Oh yeah?" said Fisher angrily. "Dead matelots. Always raises a tear."

"Tell me about it," said Dodger.

"What the fuck do you know about it, shipmate?" Fisher responded bitterly.

"Quite a bit. My bezzy oppo died in my arms on the *Cheltenham* six years back in Corporate when we were attacked. Harry Wilmott died three days ago in my arms on here down in the mess when Jumper stabbed him. That's what the fuck I know about it."

Fisher dropped his gaze and stared at the deck. "I had no idea," he said finally and almost apologetically.

"I didn't want this, Johnny," said Dodger. "I wanted Fowler to shit himself, the wardroom and Senior Rates to grow a fucking pair and something … anything to happen to stop him making our lives worse."

"Yeah, but that's not what happened. Your idea was shit. It was flawed. Topsy has the ship now and he's fucking mental."

"He mentioned he was in another mutiny?" said Dodger, hoping he'd softened Fisher's ire somewhat.

"Yes," said the Stores Accountant. "Can't recall what ship. One of the big County Class Destroyers I think. Griff, out of our mess was on the ship at the time with him. The mutiny failed and he did 56 days in Colchester nick. He was very lucky not to be kicked outside. He was minor roles in it but two of the ringleaders were booted out, and the instigator went to civvy nick for ten for it. Nobody died though ... "

Dodger's guts lurched at this prospect. As things stood, he knew he was doing time for this. It would wreck his own life and possibly kill his mum. And Louise ... what about her? Would she understand? Would she forgive him?

Would anyone forgive him?

"The Navy only kept Topsy in because he's good at his job as a Radar Plotter," added Fisher. "And he got his killicks hook back just last year. Fucking no idea why the Chief Ops made him Leader of the Seaman's messdeck. I can't think of a more nutbar dickhead. They all love him down there though."

Fisher looked back out at the wake of the *Warwick*.

"Now he's running the ship and has guns and about twenty people following him. This feels like a bad dream," said Dodger morosely.

Fisher looked back at him unsmiling. Behind his eyes was schadenfreude and no pity. "I'd ask you how we get ourselves out of this situation, but I guess you have no idea?" he said.

"No," said Dodger. "We're more prisoners now than we were with Fowler."

"Exactly. And if I am not too stupid to understand as a fucking blanket-stacker, I'd say that Hercules and the holes shot in it are basically a statement of intent, and those fuckers back in the UK get the message we look like we mean business." Fisher again looked out over the guardrails at the ocean. "I'd say right now we are now being hunted. Topsy isn't interested in talking to them either. This is going to end up being a whole lot messier and uglier unless we get rid of him and his gang."

Dodger felt like leaping into the sea. "How the fuck do we do that?" he asked.

"No idea. Spoke with one or two in his mess and they just want to get out of his way and keep their heads down very low. Almost all the ship realises we are in big shit street now."

Fisher drew a breath, sighing deeply and shaking his head. "No one is going to take Topsy on."

"What do you think he wants?"

"Fuck knows. Fame? Notoriety? We can't go on with this anyway. We're almost out of fuel, aren't we?"

"And fresh water. Ian Rees has switched off the showers and bathrooms. We've about five tons left, if that, for food and drinking. I'm not exactly sure about the rest of the kit either. No one gives much of a fuck about keeping it going. We're a diesel generator and an engine down." Dodger fished out a packet of cigarettes and offered John one, to which he declined.

"Is your mess full up with pissheads?" asked Dodger.

"Some. We didn't have that many anyway. Obviously, the Stewards have got fuck all to do and the Writers are just sat watching Top Gun, Rocky and Monty Python on the video all day. The Chefs have cleaned up their messdeck and moved back in but the scran from the galley is fucking terrible without Doc."

"Look, Johnny ..." said Dodger, breaking the spell a bit. "If anyone has any big ideas how we get ourselves out of this, count me in."

This Fouled Anchor

"I've heard this before, Dodger. What do you want? Hatches down again?" Fisher replied sarcastically. "If you think Fowler was harsh lobbing CS Gas down your grot, think what Topsy would do. And we need you lot to keep the ship alive and afloat. We're thousands of miles from any help or any land and reliant on this steel box we're sharing with a handful of pissed-up nutters to stay alive." Dodger remained silent. Fisher had a very valid point.

"We're our own prisoners now. If we get caught up with, we have to rely on the outcomes being good and us ending up in once-only survival suits and in a liferaft and a ship in range to pick us up. We still don't know if the Officers and Senior Rates have been recovered yet either. Those poor cunts could still be out there."

Chapter Twenty

Thursday 6th October 1988
London
2200

Independent Television News's iconic introduction to its ITV 'News at Ten' bulletin rolled across the nation's television screens, the animated zoom over the London skyline to position the camera facing the northernly-clockface of the UKs most notable timepiece being followed by the doom-inducing clang of its internal chime. Sir Alastair Burnett, being tonight's duty anchor, boomed out the headline with due seriousness and drama in his broadcaster's voice, "Task Force sails to quell mutiny," accompanied by stock footage of naval vessels departing from Portsmouth during the earlier Operation Corporate to retake the Falkland Islands from Argentine invasion. Typically, the editors had bent the needle of editorial accuracy and were showing aircraft carriers underway and a submarine with Harrier FRS1 jets landing and zooming past the camera. In reality, two ships, *HMS Athene* and *RFA White Rover* currently comprised the 'Task Force' mentioned with other ships, some of them well over a thousand miles away, were receiving orders to standby to dispatch if needed to provide assistance. This did not deter ITN's newshounds and Burnett followed in on the headline, again accompanied with ridiculously inaccurate and speculative footage with:

"Good evening. British Naval forces were on standby today and heading at full speed to the South Atlantic where the crew of a British warship, said to be the 4200 tonne Guided Missile Destroyer *HMS Warwick*, has mutinied and taken control of the ship. Ministers are currently in consultation with Defence Chiefs about the situation and Prime Minister Thatcher is said to be 'deeply disturbed' by the notion that one of Britain's Naval vessels is having crew problems." The programme cut back to Burnett sat in front of a screen showing a Type 22 Frigate in a high-speed turn. "Our Defence Correspondent, James Wheeler …"

Wheeler then cut in, standing outside the Ministry of Defence building in Whitehall, London in an overcoat with rain pattering down on him. "The Ministry of Defence is reeling tonight at the news that *HMS Warwick*, a Type 42 destroyer, is currently experiencing what is said by sources to be a mutiny amongst her crew. No details have yet emerged about the safety of those on board, but sources close to the Ministry have said that the Aircraft Carrier *Indomitable* (library pictures) has been despatched from her exercises in the mid-Atlantic and the frigates *Malvern* and *Rapier* (more library pictures, this time inaccurate), accompanied by a tanker are to join *Indomitable* and sail South, as soon as possible. Other unsubstantiated sources within the MoD have hinted the nuclear-powered submarine, *Sabre* is heading at full speed to the area. A statement from the Ministry is expected soon and The Prime Minister is to make a full Commons statement in the morning."

The bulletin continued, "*HMS Warwick* is a Type 42 destroyer ... equipped with ..." and continued, simply to build tension and speculation of the watching audience.

In her flat northwest of Andover, Louise found it difficult to breathe and reached for her asthma inhaler as she watched in horror ...

Junior Ratings Dining Hall
2005

Dodger and Keith were seated at a table, with Alan Theaker and another one of Topsy's 'faces' nearby. The rest of the Dining Hall was packed, with everyone again eating, this time pretty revolting attempt at 'pot mess'. Since Doc's death, food had taken a distinct downturn, and it seemed no-one could be arsed anymore. Keith chased a bit of pale grey, fatty meat around the stainless-steel platter with his fork.

"So, what do you reckon, then?" he said, looking up at Dodger, who hasn't said much since he sat down.

"I dunno, mate. I suppose ... well, I suppose we got it all wrong, eh?" Dodger hardly made eye-contact and still seemed deeply ashamed and reflective.

"Why?" Keith was at least glad he'd got a response from Dodger.

"Well ... I reckon the *Athene*'s probably sailed ... it's on its way now as we speak, despite what Topsy says. And that bollocks about the SAS, or whatever, on that Albert. What a load of dogshit. They were on Maritime Patrol. They were here to see what the score was and maybe see if ..." Dodger stopped and looked round. He could see quite a few had stopped eating and were listening to him. "… they were trying to make contact …" he continued. "… observe … not to attack."

"Reckon they've found the rafts?" asked Keith.

"Maybe. Maybe not." added Dodger. He continued eating.

"What do you reckon Fowler's told them? Reckon he's blubbed?"

"Yeah, he's probably wriggling like a worm. He'll stitch anyone he can. Trouble is, for the moment, everything he says will be Gospel. And he'll lay it on pretty thick, too." Dodger stopped eating the shit in his tray and dropped his fork into it, pulling a displeased, disgusted face.

"How do you mean?" asked one of Topsy's men.

"He'll have stitched up the Officers and Senior Rates," said Dodger. "They'll be in as much shit as us, you know."

Suddenly, Alan Theaker broke in. "I don't think they've even been picked up, you know." He lowered his voice. "You know something else? When we first put them into the rafts, I thought, 'Yeah! Fuckin' right!' and I thought that we'd just amble about near to them for a few hours, a day or so, something like that. I didn't think we'd actually leave the bastards. I thought we'd pick them up and fuck off to East Cove, sort the shit out there. I didn't think we'd sail out here." Theaker went quiet for a bit and looked down into his lap. "And when we shot at that Albert ... well ... it looks like our number's up, Keith. I'm shitting myself, I really am."

Keith chuckled nervously. "I'm scared too, fellers. So is everyone else."

Dodger spoke next. "Has Topsy threatened any of you, down the mess?" This was to Theaker, who was sniffing and still looking downwards.

"Oh, aye! He's been for a few of us," said the Able Seaman, who Dodger now concluded wasn't 'one of Topsy's men' at all and if anything wanted to switch sides. "He went for Tim Gooding with a Stanley ... and he's had the nine mil out a few times! Why? Has he had you?"

Dodger pointed to the raised mound of flesh just below his eye and the black scab that had formed there.

"Trouble is, though. Topsy's got a lot of the lads behind him. They've got the tools. Some of the lads in the mess want to do him ... but no-one's got the guts!" The Able Seaman

This Fouled Anchor

looked at Keith, then at Theaker, then at Dodger. He was right.

"We've been in this situation before, shipmate!" said Dodger to Keith, who nodded back, bleakly.

"Tell you what," Keith announced, placing his own fork down in the tray of sludge. "If the fighting starts, I'm over the side, mate, straight-off. I don't wanna die. I'm not putting my arse on the line for no-one. Not for him, anyway."

Theaker looked up. "How are we doing for fuel, Dodger?"

"Grim. According to the tankies, a day and a half. After that, we're sucking fumes!"

"Christ!" said Theaker, his voice a bit wobbly with desperation. We might as well jack the whole lot in, now. We're fucked! It's hopeless!"

At almost the same time, the Brigadier Mike Jones sat in Commander Phil Chapman's Office. With them were the three crew members of the C130 and their payload of Signals and intelligence staff with additional advisers and Logistics staffers.

"... so, *Kilo*-Class? You are sure about that, aren't you?" Jones said to the defence intelligence analyst, whose name he'd forgot but knew he played golf from a previous encounter at a drinks party in Port Stanley. "Because if there's any doubt, then you must understand, this could change the whole complexion of the situation."

Chapman's second-in-charge, Lt Cdr 'Banjo' West, himself a submariner, answered for the analyst. "No, sir. I'm sure. It's Russian. It's Kilo-Class."

"Banjo's right, sir. I've flown over these babies too many times to be mistaken," added Pearson. "They're up to no good, sir."

Jones paused, frowning and looked down at the photos, slowly shaking his head. He sat down at his desk and picked up the phone, still looking at the photos in slow sequence and pressed six numbers. On answering, Jones said, "Ah, yes. Corporal Carter! Get me the secure line to MoD Whitehall. Yes. Yes. The Assistant Chief of Defence Staff. Yes." He then looked up, hoping to see one solitary doubtful face amongst those looking back at him. There was none. All had 'do it' written on them.

Chapter Twenty-One

HMS *Athene*. North-West of South Georgia
Saturday 8th October 1988
0710

On the Bridge of the Exocet-Leander Class Frigate, the Captain sat silently observing the gathering operation. His crew had been extensively briefed, and he'd had about fifty-five minutes of real sleep in the past forty-eight hours. Last night had been head-thuddingly tense, both gameplaying this situation with his departmental heads, speaking with Command back in the Falklands and also with both Whitehall and Northwood on secure lines, again easily tapped by the Soviet Union and now the United States of America. The Soviets, for their part, retired their submarine to a distance of fifteen kilometres and 150 metres depth, surfacing occasionally to check the traffic via periscope and electronic radar detection. They had dived again when they picked up

Athene's Type 974 navigation radar, reporting the arrival of the ship on station.

"Action Lynx, Action Lynx!" announced the Officer of the Watch over the main broadcast. Back aft on the flightdeck, *Athene*'s helicopter, dubbed 'Tootsie' with a small cartoon owl painted on either side of her nose, lifted off noisily with two live Sea Skua missiles underslung of each cabin door on their weapons pylons. Dawn was grey and just breaking and the machine rattled down the side of the ship and banked outwards as the ship changed course downtrack forty-five kilometres from *Warwick*. The strategy had changed overnight and after a fraught Defence inner circle meeting and telephone conversation with the Secretary of State, Prime Minister and Defence Chiefs, a way ahead had been agreed. As Tootsie left the deck, Margaret Thatcher was speaking with Her Majesty the Queen in her reception office at Windsor Castle after a very high-speed dispatch along the M4 with squadrons of blue-lit motorcycles accompanying her.

0716

A few Stokers sat in the darkened mess square watching pornography on the ship's video system in the twilight. They had blank expressions with the tedium. Nige McDonnell, slowly raised his beer can to his mouth and stopped. He grinned, watching the action. He then paused, his eyes not moving from the screen and without moving his gaze took a swig and a drag of his cigarette. Suddenly the television went blank, and the emergency lighting switched on, illuminating their faces. Nige and his messmates were still blankly staring at the television.

"Hey! I was enjoying that! Some fucker go put ten pee in the meter," said Nige.

Up in the Machinery Control Room both J1 and M2 Diesel Generators had simultaneously tripped, robbing the ship of all electrical power. The ship was designed to still move under her own propulsion power without this but steering and all other ship management systems were gone, until someone started the standby generator and closed the breakers to resupply the electrical distribution system. Mick Barnes was trusted with this, and he'd initiated the start on the standby, but it had refused and whilst he was busy cancelling the cacophony of audible and visible alarms on the main panel, he called out to Tanzy Lee who was his stoker of the watch, "Tanzy! Go down the After Space, will you? See what's happened to that generator! Carry out a local start if you can …"

Tanzy was unimpressed, as ever. Snatching up his ear protection he shot back at Mick, "Aw! Fuckin' hell! Can't some other twat do this? I've been on watch since last night. The mess is toppers with bastards who haven't had a go yet!"

Mick gave Tanzy a meaningful stare. "Just fucking do it, will you? And stop dripping. You're like a fucking septic arsehole."

Tanzy skulked away, outside into the passageway. Pretty soon he'd got the generator back on and Mick had supplies restored, but Tanzy informed him that the diesel ready use tank supplying that machine was down to 250 gallons, just over half-full. Mick scrabbled about to transfer fuel to it from the already-almost-empty diesel service tanks.

Main Communications Office

0800

Topsy, Alan Theaker and another one of Topsy's trusted guards are listened to a crackly World Service bulletin on the Short-Wave receiver speaker. The presenter had a wonderful, fruity BBC voice.

"This is London. It's Ten Hours." This was followed by the time-pips. Then he continued.

"Here is the news. Britain is sending a Task Force to the South Atlantic to quell a mutiny on board one of her warships. *HMS Warwick*, a Type 42 anti-aircraft destroyer is currently one hundred and fifty miles north of the island of South Georgia, scene of the origin of the Falklands crisis, six and a half years ago.

The British missile frigate *Athene* is said to have put to sea from the naval facility of East Cove, on East Falkland and is heading out to South Georgia."

"Bollocks," said Theaker, sounding distinctly worried.

"The precise cause of the mutiny is as yet unknown, but sources within the Ministry of Defence have hinted that some of the senior staff from the ship have been cast adrift in the lifeboats, but this has not been confirmed. Prime Minister Thatcher today made a statement to a hushed House of Commons giving scant outlines of the incident, and limited details of a way ahead although in a press conference later, Defence Secretary George Younger remained tight-lipped and promised updates as events developed. Opposition Leaders were unanimous in their support for the Premier in bringing the problem to a swift conclusion. Mr Kinnock said, a short while ago … "

Topsy broke away and looked at his compatriots. "It doesn't mean nothin'!" he said, dismissively, and he patted a reassuring hand on Theaker's shoulder. "Believe me. They can't touch us. We'll be alright. You're safe with me."

Next door in the Operations Room, Able Seaman Foulkes again sat by his electronic warfare panel. The UAA1 array at the top of the main mast was switched on and monitoring outward for radar frequencies hitting the ship, giving forewarning of anything nearby. Suddenly it was alarming. Foulkes checked the display and reached for a clip file just as Topsy and Alan Theaker appeared behind him. The Able Seaman didn't really need the clip file, he knew what frequency, energy and bandwidth this radar was.

"What's up?" asked Topsy, leaning in.

"It's Seaspray, Tops," said Foulkes. "From a Lynx. They've found us, Topsy. They've fucking found us!"

"Shit!" said Topsy and moved across to the Principal Warfare Officer's plot where a Main Broadcast microphone was. He picked it up, pressing the Main Broadcast Alarm before announcing, "Hands to Action Stations, Hands to Action Stations!" he said.

Elsewhere in the ship, the remainder barely alive or interested struggled into their overalls and to their positions. Mick Barnes had been relieved by Ian Rees in the Machinery Control Room and passed Atky in the passageway.

"It's a fucking wind up, yeah?" said Atky, pulling up his overalls over his massive shoulders.

"No mate! Buzz is the *Athene*'s not far away. We're done for! Best get your lifejacket on shippers."

Sixteen miles away in the cockpit of Tootsie, an alarm light lit on the Flight Observer's console. He keyed his comms switch, "*Warwick*'s active," he said, indicating that their target had her 1022 long-range air search on. No sign so far of *Warwick*'s tactical targeting 996 radar yet and certainly no indication of the helicopter being lit up by either the 909 targeting radar nor the Vulcan Phalanx Close in Weapons System with its search and tracking radar and 3000 rounds-per-minute M61A2 six barrelled rotary cannon. At least *Warwick* now knew they were there.

The Observer keyed his Sea Skua target indication panel and selected the port missile which returned all the signals he needed to tell him it was ready and had the information needed.

"Terminal Height ... one five. We're in range. Permission for weapon release?" he said.

"Standby," said the Flight Commander, next to him and he adjusted the nose on the Lynx slightly and dropped fifteen feet toward the waves whilst still retaining forward motion of 155 knots. "Spear, this is Owl. Target acquired. Permission to release Sword."

Back in *Athene*'s darkened Operations Room, the Captain nodded through his anti-flash hood to the Principal Warfare Officer (Air) who keyed his switch. "Command approved," he replied.

The Observer's gloved index finger stabbed the 'release' button, and the helicopter lurched slightly as it was freed of the deadweight 145kg of the missile. It continued forward underneath the helicopter, dropping toward the sea and then its booster motor ignited, lighting the surface and the underside of the aircraft in a pink/orange glow. Then it streaked away, arcing to starboard and then slightly to port as its radar went active and found the hull of *Warwick* up ahead.

Dodger descended the ladder in the After Engine Room and took up position between the two Rolls Royce Tyne gas turbine engine modules. Both were running and the ship was manoeuvring port to starboard for some reason. Jumper Crossley was already down in the machinery space and offered Dodger a cheery thumbs up. This was interpreted he'd already carried out the 'State One Checks' to make the machinery ready for any incoming action. Jumper sat on an upper ladder, his legs dangling. Dodger could see he had no socks on inside his boots. Dodger donned a cabled headset and spoke. "MCR, After Engine Room. LMEM Long, MEM Crossley, closed up. There was no response. Over the headset he heard broken comms from the Forward Engine Room but couldn't work out who it was down there.

This Fouled Anchor

Jumper took out a packet of Embassy Number 1, slid out a cigarette and lit it. He was sat under a huge painted sign that said, 'NO SMOKING'. Dodger waved to get Jumper's attention. When he looked, Dodger mouthed, "Where's Nige?" Jumper shrugged and carried on puffing his fag. He then offered Dodger one. Dodger crossed the gap between them and took one, lighting it from Jumper's glowing end. Man, that felt fucking good.

On the Bridge, Topsy was amongst several mutineers. He was anxiously staring out of the starboard aft Bridge window, trying to pick out something, anything. Jon Fisher appeared up through the hatch from the deck below. He had tears in his eyes.

"Topsy, for fuck's sake! They've found us. Let's give it up now, eh? Let's give it up?" he yelled, almost sobbing. Topsy crossed the bridge and defiantly picked up the intercom microphone. Staring at Fisher he said, "Upperdeck crews. Target approaching. Starboard quarter. It's a Lynx. Engage when ready."

Fisher screamed, "No!" and lunged at Topsy, both falling to the floor. A struggle ensued with attempts at gouging eyes and half-deflected punches. Other men moved to break it up, but Topsy wrestled a free arm and pulled out his Browning 9mm from his pocket. He jammed the muzzle into Fisher's throat. Fisher and the rest of the men froze. Topsy's finger tightened on the trigger and the gun went off with a loud crack, peppering the Bridge and its occupants with blood and tissue. Fisher's body, now with a loosely attached head, slumped forward, the exited round caught LPTI Sewell in the upper thigh, and he released the helm dropping sideways and calling out in agony. The rest of the mutineers shared shocked expressions. Topsy fought off Fisher's limp body.

From the side of the Bridge, Alan Theaker screamed, "Shit, fellers! Missile inbound, green one-two-zero!"

The missile crossed the line of sight of the gunners as they frantically tried to shoot at it. It rocketed past, ricochetting off the deck and burying itself into the side of the ship, destroying the starboard Olympus gas turbine air intakes and several surrounding compartments, it's armour piercing warhead ballooning out a vast sphere of flame, debris and smoke.

In the After Engine Room, Dodger looked up and flinched knowingly as the ship shuddered under the explosion. He cast Jumper a fearful look. The lights dimmed, flickered, and half of them went out. There was a further bang, and a column of flame erupted from a fan trunking directly above Jumper's head where he sat. It enveloped him momentarily and then retracted. Jumper, his skin and clothes now aflame danced a macabre, agonising jig. He pitched forward onto the deck plating, still wriggling and screeching and Dodger moved toward him, grabbing an extinguisher and operated it, playing the foam onto the stricken man. The shock and terror in Dodger's face was evident. He threw down the extinguisher and knelt by Jumper. Dodger pulled him up into his arms. Jumper was taking short, sharp, hacking breaths, through the complete mess that was his face. His eyes, nose, mouth were unrecognisable, and some of his lifejacket had melted, fusing skin with plastic. Dodger started to weep.

"It's okay … Jumper … you poor bastard …"

Topsy threw the lumpen corpse of Jon Fisher off his body. Covered in his blood and body parts, he raised to his feet and crossed the Bridge in front of stunned participants. He grabbed the Conning 1 microphone and keyed the button. "MCR, Bridge. Get this fucking ship moving …" Those around him were paralysed and themselves moving in slow motion. Jon Fisher's body lay twitching and still pumping blood through a chasm where once his lower jaw and base of his skull was. It was horrific. Topsy pulled Sewell out of his chair onto the deck as he kept yelping and dragged another Able Seaman over, bundling him into the Quartermaster's chair. "Steer the fucking ship!" he commanded and showed the terrified AB his pistol.

Down in the Machinery Control Room, Mick Barnes picked himself off the floor in the smoky room. Others around him had panicked, startled looks on their faces. Mick rubbed his eyes and replied via the intercom. Alarms and warning enunciators were beep-beeping. He looked next door into the Damage Control Headquarters, but it was empty. The people meant to be there had scarpered.

"Bridge, MCR!" he coughed into the microphone. "We're … we've lost all engines. The main engines are … gone! What's hit us?"

"A missile!" responded Topsy. "Get the ship moving! Now!"

"Roger, dodge!" replied Mick. But really, he didn't have a clue what to do. One of the cruise engines was still running but unresponsive. 'Tripped' lights were everywhere and he could smell an electrical fire too.

Downstairs in the Aft Engine Room, Dodger heard one of the Tyne cruise engines roll down to a stop. He laid Jumper down and took a conscious look at the surroundings then at Jumper, lowly moaning in his doomed existence. Dodger uncontrollably blubbered and then started up the ladders to get out of the machinery space. He took a cursory look back at the top before he left. He saw Jumper rise, flail around briefly, then fall forward under the guardrails into the bilges, just his feet sticking out. The legs twitched horribly and then were still. Dodger continued up the ladder and out onto 2 deck. He had to get out.

Outside another Sea Skua missile bore down on the ship. It winged, unmolested into the after part of the ship, carving a swage through the outer bulkhead before detonating inside the Petty Officer's messdeck and upwards into the air weapons magazine where eight Stingray torpedoes and ten Sea Skua missiles sat. All of them detonated sequentially within a second. The explosion sent a dulling shock wave through the ship blowing out tons of steel, fittings and most of the remaining ships company in the after part of *Warwick*. The debris hurtled hundreds of feet into the air outwards, and the aft part of the ship buckled and folded horrendously, the internal shockwave blasting doors off their hinges and leaving a gaping wound into which cold seawater poured in. Both propulsion shafts seized and stopped as the ship deformed, and the remaining hangar and flightdeck collapsed downwards killing everyone in the aft sections who were not already vapourised by the magazine explosion. Dodger was four sections forward of this and was thrown bodily into the air and up the passageway. The whole of the ship's electrical supply now failed, lighting, ventilation, power all now winding down, killing the ship. Battery operated emergency lamps came on and the air was filled with fire, smoke and sparks. Dodger assembled himself and was joined by Mick Barnes who had escaped the Machinery Control Room. Down the passageway toward the stern, from the direction of the last missile hit, there was a hint of fire and muffled shouts, cries, screams.

"What the fuck's happening?" screamed Mick, in massive stress.

"We've been hit!" replied Dodger. "Look!" He pointed aft, down the passageway.

Coming out of the orange glow-gloom were the forms of three people, staggering, blindly. The front one was Atky, his antiflash hood and overalls smouldering. He was dragging a body, unconscious or dead. He reached a fire hydrant in front of Dodger and Mick and dropped the body to the deck. Atky picked up the firefighting nozzle and swung open the stop valve. A lame dribble emitted from the end.

"Bastard!" he said. Atky picked up the body again by the scruff and started to drag it. He stopped, noticing Dodger and Mick, his black skin glistening with sweat.

"Fucking hell! Help me, for fuck's sake!" he said in desperation. "We've got to help them. Let's …"

Mick noticed that the body Atky was dragging had no legs and was very dead. Dodger grabbed Atky by the lapels of his overalls. "Let's get up-top!" he said. "The ship's fucked! *We're* fucked!"

They all agreed, and they made their way forward, past other damaged areas. They came across two bodies, one a chef, the other, just the bottom half of a person in overalls sprawled across him. Both were seriously burned, mutilated and dead. Eventually they headed up a ladder, and Dodger, being last, cast a glance aft, down the passageway. All he could see were flames, and they were advancing. Dodger quickly ascended the ladder.

Once out onto the upper deck, it was cold, dazzling sunshine, and they shielded their eyes from it. In the far distance somewhere, a helicopter hovered. From the cockpit the observer studies the men emerging from various hatches and doors. Some are donning the orange survival suits and lifejackets. One man leaped straight into the sea, without both. The Flight Observer keyed his microphone to speak directly to *Athene*.

"Spear, this is Owl. Ah … they're abandoning! Yap! They're donning once-onlys! I think it's all done for them. There's one … two impacts … Jesus … they're on fire and the ship is settling aft. There's going to be some casualties!"

Down in the After Auxiliary Machinery Room, the impact of the second Sea Skua had buckled and torn a large series of holes in the starboard side of the ship, below the waterline. Tanzy was tending to a large split in the side of the ship's outer bulkhead, where the sea was gushing in over his body. His flesh became waxy and pale, and as he tried to hammer softwood wedges into the crack, his blows getting less and less effective. He was weakening. He gasped and took in an unintentional mouthful of water. Very quickly the level of freezing water in the compartment rose to his shoulders and Tanzy visibly faltered. His breaths were short and sudden, and he was soon overwhelmed. His head went forward into the water flowing out of the split. The level rose above the crack and swirled. There was no sign of Tanzy. He was gone.

The ship started to settle by the stern and then list to starboard. Out on the starboard waist, Dodger, Atky and Mick were making their way aft. Three gunshots rang out and the men staggered, blindly shocked at not just escaping a sinking ship, but now being shot at. One bullet ricocheted off the deck. They broke into a run and came under the cover of an overhanging boat sponson. There were more men cowering there, some in once-only suits. Topsy was firing blindly at men on the upperdeck. Two men lay dead where he stood above them at his feet.

"Bastards! I put my neck on the line for you cunts!" he screamed, quickly reloading. "If I go down … you fuckers are coming with me!"

Dodger hunkered under the sponson. Alan Theaker shuffled over. "What's going on?" Dodger said.

Theaker was almost over the ledge. "It's Topsy! He's lost it! We launched a liferaft, and he shot holes in it! We're all gonna fuckin' die, Dodge! We're going down with the fuckin' ship!"

An Able Seaman who Dodger recognised as one of Topsy's cohort chipped in. "He's shot two lads from the mess on the boatdeck. They're dead, Dodger!" The kid was crying now. "He blew one of their fucking heads off. And he's shot Johnny Fisher on the Bridge. They were having a scrap, so Topsy fucking shot him."

Dodger looked at Atky, who widened his eyes in a 'I got that' gesture. The ship lurched to starboard and hardly recovered. It was clear it was going down and if they weren't quick, so were they.

"Right!" Dodger said. "We gotta get out from under here, or we're dead." He looked up. Above him was a liferaft cradle, with the painter line to connect it to the ship and trigger automatic inflation dangling within reach. He reached up and pulled the line. He swung on it.

"What you doing?" said Atky.

"Give us a hand, will you shipmate?"

Atky leant his considerable strength and weight to Dodger's exertions. They both pulled about two metres of line down then suddenly the raft in the cradle above them exploded open and self-inflated where it sat. It was just the cue needed. Topsy, from the Bridge wing, fired on the raft, puncturing it. The men trapped below scurried aft whilst Topsy's attention was drawn. He noticed the last man, the Able Seaman, and fired two rounds at him.

The men reached the cover and safety of the upperdeck cross passage, blocked from Topsy's sight. The stern of the ship was nearly submerged, and Dodger could see the extent of the damage of the magazine explosion. In the cross passage, there were more men, trapped by the gunshots. The ship again lurched sharply to starboard, and the water gently lapped over the deck edge. The men panicked. Time was running out.

"Shit! What are we gonna do?" cried Theaker.

Dodger waved most of the men in in a huddle. "Look, fellers! We'll all go over the upper side in groups of three. If he shoots at you, keep going. Slide down the side of the ship and get under the stabilisers. When the ship goes down, get the fuck away from it. Stay together in the water." Everyone, without exception, nodded at this plan.

"Dodger, there's no more once-only suits," said Mick Barnes, who'd appeared from nowhere. "The rest are all up by the bridge in the lockers. We'll all freeze to fucking death!"

Thinking quick, Dodger said to the men, "Everyone in once-onlys first, then. You three … yeah … you … you and, er … you mate … you're first. Okay?" He turned to Mick and Atky, bringing them in a touch. "Look. Most of us will freeze whatever. I can't see any shipping about, and by the looks of it, we'll be in the water for longer than we can take … but it's our only hope. The only thing we can expect is that the remaining rafts break free like they're designed to do and self-inflate. If they don't … we're fucked!"

Dodger then turned to the four men in the orange suits. "Ready? Don't stop, lads. Just leg it, yeah?"

They all nodded back. It was clear they were all shitting themselves. The ship told them all she was dying and rolled lazily.

"Go!" shouted Dodger, and men scurried clumsily uphill. They reached the guardrail and climbed over. Suddenly, they were gone. No shots.

"Next three, no … make it four. Yeah. Ready?" He checked up, toward the Bridge.

"Go!" and they went. There was a crack of a gunshot, but it missed. All the men made it up and over. The only ones left now were Mick, Atky, Dodger and the young Able Seaman in his once-only. They cast fearful glances at each other.

"Ready?" said Dodger.

"Yeah!" said Atky.

"Let's fucking do it!" said Mick.

All four made a desperate dash uphill on the sloping deck for the guard rail. First over was Mick, who cleared it almost without touching it. Atky did similar, closely followed by the Able Seaman, but his plastic suit, baggy and awkward, snagged on a fastening on the guard rail and as he jumped for safety, he was snared and fell back against the outside of the stanchion. There he dangled, his feet bicycling for a foothold, his hands scrabbling for purchase.

"... n-n-no! Ah ... uh ... Dodger ... help, for ... fuck's sake!" he screamed. "Help me!"

Just then there was the crack of a gunshot. The Able Seaman's thigh exploded in a shower of blood as the round passed clean through it. He screamed, tortuously. Dodger, who had by now made it alongside the Able Seaman and was just about to let go and slide down the ship's side stopped and turned. He looked upward straight into the eyes of Topsy, who had made it down from the Bridge to one deck above the stricken pair, ten feet away. Topsy was smiling satisfactorily and raised the gun to point at Dodger. Dodger looked at the water, and Atky and Mick swimming for cover. He was caught. He reached out, not taking his eyes off Topsy and yanked at Able Seaman's suit, defiantly. It tore, ripped some more and the man fell a bit. The suit snagged again. Dodger yanked at it; his hands covered in blood. This time it separated and Able Seaman fell, sliding down the grey ship's side headlong into the water. Dodger watched Topsy slowly zero his sights on him, smiling. The ship's deck angle steepened, and Dodger closed his eyes, ready to die. All he could think about was Louise.

At the top of the mainmast in his hide, Petty Officer Crawford zeroed in on Topsy's head. It was an awkward angle. He settled, exhaled and squeezed the trigger, the high-velocity round hitting Topsy in the base of his neck, travelling through his body and exiting under his right arm, taking a lot of body parts and tissue with it. Topsy grunted and staggered against a locker. He gave a startled, wheezy cough and fell to the deck, still, as the consciousness and life drained out of him.

Dodger opened his eyes and looked up at the mainmast and then let go falling, sliding into the sea. He hit the water, submerging and surfacing quickly, rocketing upwards out in shock, gasping for breath. It was very, very fucking cold.

"Sh-h-it!" he gasped and tried to fire up his limbs to swim over to the exposed stabiliser fin. The other survivors were sheltering under it, treading water and shivering. From where he was, Dodger could see one or two other survivors in the water down by the stern, which was now submerged. There were agonising creaks, groans and thuds from within the ship, and assorted muffled booms and crashes as equipment and fittings toppled or became unseated. The other survivors splashed toward Dodger and the others, shouting, yelling, gasping. The ship rolled sharply onto its side, exposing Atky and the others. Dodger tried to speak to them, but the cold had control of his mouth.

"It's o-o-k-k-ay, fellllers! Someb-somebody shot Topsy! H-h-he's ... f-kin dead!"

Everyone gingerly paddled toward Dodger, with the swell bobbing them all. *Warwick* settled in her position, her barnacle-encrusted hull dripping silently. Atky reached Dodger first.

"J-jesus! I'm farhu-u-ckin freezing! Wh-wh-who shot Topsy?"

"Dunno!" Dodger replied. He could feel the cold numbing his face and extremities now. All he had on were overalls and his working rig. He could feel one of his boots had loosened too.

Athene's helicopter swung in low and dropped its rescue sling to a survivor further aft. The man put it over his body, and he was winched upward, painfully slowly.

"This is gonn-nn-na take all f-fucking day!" Mick complained. "My legs are going numb. I can't feel my f-huckin hands."

Another man is rescued, then another, then the helicopter banked away. The men got desperate.

"Oi! Oi! Come b-back, you fucking bastards! Come back!" yelled Atky. Dodger could tell, swimming wasn't Atky's best subject. He turned to Dodger, his head barely breaking the surface and his arms flailing uselessly. "I can't stand it much longer. I'm d-dying."

Mick splashed over and pulled Atky up a bit whilst treading water. "Well, it sure ain't Montego Bay, eh, negro?"

Atky found strength and rallied. He was fucking furious. "If-if I had the f-fucking strength, I'd kick your f-fucking head in, fat boy!" he cried out.

"Just make sure you make it Atky, and I'll give you a hand," said Dodger. The Able Seaman bobbed over to them. He was barely conscious, and his face was white with shock. His head dipped beneath the water, and he came back up, gasping.

"Hey lads," said Dodger. "Lend us a hand ..." and they all crowded around the man and held him up. It was evident even their own strength was sapping.

"Where are all the others?" said Mick. They looked around but found that they were alone. The ship again made dreadful, agonising groaning noises, jarring, juddering shrieks and thumps from within as she rolled further away from them.

"It looks like she's going" called Dodger, fearfully.

Just then, a warship appeared from around the stern of the *Warwick*. It quickly came alongside and, with a roar and shudder, slowed to a stop. A launch was lowered, and it sped out to them. Three men manned the launch, the one at the front was carrying a rifle, aimed at Atky, Dodger, Mick and the Able Seaman. Dodger was struggling himself now, his kicking had slowed to a stroll, and each wavelet now washed over his head. He suddenly felt warm and calm.

"F-fuckin' h-hurrry up-p-p, you bastards!" called Atky.

The boat got alongside the survivors and the helmsman and other crewmember hoisted the Able Seaman in. Dodger could see the damage to the man's thigh, but the bleeding had almost stopped. Mick got up next, then Atky, then Dodger.

One of the crew members issued blankets to them and Dodger slowly huddled into his, resting his face on the gunwhale of the boat. The crew member checked each rescuee in turn.

"You okay? Any injuries? Sure?" he said. Dodger, Atky and Mick shook their heads, but internally rejoiced in being allowed to live. Dodger begins to shiver uncontrollably as the boat turned back toward *Athene*. He looked out over the swell at the hull of *Warwick*, which now has its bow out of the water. The Coxswain of the boat spoke.

"She's going!" he said, almost mournfully.

Warwick's bow rose vertically, paused briefly, then sank linearly and quickly into a halo of spray, foam, bubbles and flotsam. Dodger watched unblinking.

Chapter Twenty-Two

The seaboat carrying Dodger, Atky, Mick and the injured Seaman came alongside the *Athene* and the survivors were manhandled up the accommodation ladder, where another armed guard was waiting, this time in DPM camouflage gear looking purposeful.

"Come, on! This way. Aft! Everyone, this way! Back to the hanger! Fucking move it!" he called.

The survivors made their way aft, Dodger, now bootless on one foot, his wet sock slapping the deck. He was still damned cold. The Able Seaman was struggling with consciousness, held up on the shoulders of Mick and Atky. As they entered the hanger, Dodger caught sight of the helicopter winching what looked to be a dead body from the water, above the bubbles still rising from the wreck of *Warwick* still making its lonely way to the seabed three kilometres below. He stopped, shocked. There were more than a dozen floating corpses in the sea, aft of *Athene*.

This Fouled Anchor

"This way! Keep fucking moving! That's right!" shouted the guard, again.

Dodger and the men made their way to the back of the hanger where about twenty other survivors were congregated, and *Athene*'s Master-at-Arms was supervising their handling. There appeared to be no sign of anyone else from Dodger's mess. Atky and Mick lowered the Able Seaman to the deck, whence a couple of the *Athene*'s ship's company appeared, dressed in white surcoats with a huge red cross emblazoned on the front. They tended to the Able Seaman who was close to unconsciousness. Dodger felt the ship shudder and get under way. Looking out of the hanger door, he could still see the helicopter winching bodies up. Mick sidled over to Petty Officer Crawford, stood nearby.

"How the …?" he began.

"Shut your fucking mouth, arsehole!" cut back Crawford icily.

Athene's Master-at-Arms caught site of Crawford talking to Mick and burst forth aggressively. "Oi, you two!" he yelled. "Button it, before I button it for you!"

He turned to the twenty or so former members of *Warwick*'s ship's staff.

"I'll remind you all now, to remain silent. I'll make this quite clear. I don't give a flying fuck what happened on *Warwick*. Not yet anyway. It ain't gonna happen on here. For the record, you are all under arrest under Section Eight of the Naval Discipline Act, parts a, b and c. You will give your name, rate and service number to the Leading Regulator over here and then proceed below to the sickbay for a thorough examination. Any questions? No? Carry on."

The MAA left. There were three armed guards, and a whole load of other members of *Athene*'s ship staff watching over the mutineers, gawping at them. They didn't look happy, at all.

1205

Dodger, Atky and Mick were sat amongst twenty-five other surviving mutineers in the bleak Junior Ratings Dining Hall. All were now wearing brand-new overalls and had just showered and changed, again under observation and in silence. All had boots on but no socks. No-one was talking. An armed guard sat separate.

The Master-at-Arms appeared, closely followed by *Athene*'s First Lieutenant and two other officers. Finally, another armed guard entered, then quietly closed the door behind him. He remained stood.

The MAA and Officers sat at a table in front of the mutineers. The MAA shuffled some papers out of a file, found his notebook and turned to a page. He read the points succinctly and clearly, in a 'police officer' manner.

"Right. If I can have your attention, please. Thank you." He looked sternly across at the mutineers, eyeing each in turn.

"I'm here to let you know what is going to happen when we get back to the Falklands. Once we get there, there is a great deal of work to find out the reasons and what occurred – but let it be said now, no-one is apportioning blame to anyone, just yet. That is the job for the Service Investigation Branch, and I'm not even going to start to get to grips with it. That's their job, not mine, and I don't envy them."

He paused, looked down and then looked back at the mutineers. "A lot of you may be feeling the effects of shock and feeling upset. If that's the case, see the doc, he'll be able to help you. If you feel the need to talk to someone about the incidents, then I'm afraid, the only person you will be able to talk to is myself, and then only in an interview and under caution. Both the Captain and I recognise the importance of capturing every piece of information about what happened. If you are caught speaking to anyone else, we will view that very seriously. Your position in the inquiry could be implicated and the chances of your statements holding out could be jeopardised. The ship's company of HMS *Athene* have been strictly briefed not to converse with any of the protagonists, and to report any attempt to communicate, and what is said." He paused again, just the background whuzz of the ship's ventilation cut the silence.

"Does everyone understand? Anyone got any … any questions?" Dodger felt numb, and felt like crying, a lot.

"Right," continued the Master-at-Arms. "We are two days from East Cove. You'll all be billeted down in messdecks on camp-beds. You will all be escorted everywhere and will eat separately and earlier than *Athene*'s ship staff. The Leading Regulator will assign you when we leave this place. One more thing … you all … all remain under arrest."

1946

Dodger was setting up his bed for the night on the floor between bunks in a gulch in *Athene*'s Stokers' mess which was a shabby downgrade from 3 November mess on *Warwick*. His resting place for the night was a wire-framed, canvas camp bed and he had a sleeping bag also, which stunk. At the end of the gulch was a young Seaman from *Athene*'s ship's staff, assigned to guard him. Neither spoke to each other as Dodger busied himself. He looked haggard, drawn and in need of some sleep. Eventually he stripped naked and slid into the bag, snuggled down, rubbed his eyes, blinked once or twice, then was fast asleep in moments.

2330

Suddenly Dodger was snapped awake in the darkened gulch and surrounded by largely semi-naked strangers. Fear was on his startled face. All of them were in various stages of drunkenness. One of them, a fat bloke dressed in a Wolverhampton Wanderers team shirt was the first to speak.

"Oi ... oi! Wake up, you twat!"

Dodger kept the sleeping bag tight up to his face but showed the bloke he was awake.

"Er ... alright, mate!" said the man, who had a thick Black Country accent. "Er ... so ... erm ... me and the lads, like ... we were just wondering, like, what happened on there ... eh?"

Dodger was still fearful. He'd been told not to talk, and this lot didn't look friendly. He was in a lot of shit and didn't want any more. "Go away," he said. "Leave me alone, please."

Opposite, an ugly, part-naked Stoker hung from his bunk. "Aw, come on, shipmate!" he said, aggressively. "Fucking speak up then, you cunt!"

Dodger looked down the gulch for the guard. He was gone. "Look, I'm not to talk to anyone. You all know that. Now fuck off!" he said.

The Brummie straightened up and angrily lashed out with his bare foot, catching Dodger full in the face. Dodger was stunned and curled up into a protective ball. There was a huge cheer from those assembled. Brum made a few more attempts at assaulting Dodger in his sleeping bag before three or four of his messmates dragged him off.

"Alright, Brum … leave him, eh?" said one.

"Yeah, he's had enough. Let's have another beer, eh?" said another, pushing him back.

"Never touched him. Deserves it anyway!" protested Brum. "Bastard! Fuckin' bastard!"

Dodger emerged from his protection. Brum's kick had busted his lip open inside and his nose was bleeding a bit. The ugly Stoker still hung from his bunk.

"You're in a world of shit, shipmate!" he said, mockingly, chuckling and shaking his head. "You and all the others. What made you fucking do it, anyway? Jesus! What a shower of cunts."

The sentry reappeared at the end of the gulch with a tin of beer in his hand. Dodger assumed the loaded rifle he'd been given was elsewhere in the mess square, full of drunken sailors pissed off at having their return home curtailed. "E-everything alright?" he said, meekly. He didn't get a reply. He went back to the rowdy party in the mess square, where Brum could be heard getting rather irate, once again.

The ugly Stoker continued, obviously on a roll now. "I mean, we all get pissed off with the pigs on here ... but, dropping the hatches ... ha! Never heard anything like it, shipmate. I tell you!"

Dodger settled himself, tasting his blood and trying to make himself disappear. Ugly Stoker then said, "Fuckin' ridiculous! Besides, we could be home by now, for God's sake. Now we'll have to wait for months to get another fucking ship down here. Everybody's wild about it. Think about all the plans you've fucked up. People aren't happy, I can tell ya."

He then became sinister and threatening. "Tell you something. I hope you all get fucking hammered for this. Pete Dent, the reggie on here. He reckons you'll get banged up in a civvy nick ... probably ten year or so. Oh aye! The lads on here reckon you lot are a right bunch of cunts. 'Specially as you were so far from home. I mean, where were you fucking going, eh? South Pole?" Ugly paused, waiting for an answer Dodger was never going to give him. "Nah, shipmate, you were on to a loser from the kick-off. The chief in the Ops Room reckons there was a Rusky sub following you. You fuckers were going to hand the ship over to them cunts, weren't you? You crafty, fucking bastards."

Ugly Stoker slid out of his bunk, stepped around Dodger and went round to the mess square, where Dodger could hear him announce the last accusation to those assembled. Brum went fucking mental and raced round towards Dodger, only to be stopped again by more of his messmates. Finally, his drunken struggles subsided, and he retreated back to his beer.

Dodger could hear him. "It's alright! I'm alright!" he said. "Fuckin' leave me alone!"

Dodger pulled the sleeping bag up across his face, leaving just his wary eyes out. He stared at the sentry, who had reappeared. The sentry beamed benignly back at him and raised his tin of beer.

This Fouled Anchor

Chapter Twenty-Three

Monday 10th October 1988

0900

Dodger sat in the messdeck gulch, on his rear. He was smoking a cigarette, getting scant comfort from its contents and flipping the residue into an empty Pepsi Cola can. At the other end of the gulch was a fresh sentry, who was also smoking. They eyed each other on and off for a full 30 seconds before the main broadcast interrupted their competition.

"D'yer'hear there!" barked the main broadcast. "All members of *HMS Warwick* ship's company, muster in the hanger for helo departure to Mount Pleasant Airfield."

Dodger sighed, and looked at the sentry, who managed a weak smile. Dodger rose slowly and made his way toward the exit ladder, leaving the camp bed and sleeping bag unmade. Fuck 'em. Both ascended into the passageway and aft, along toward the ladder up to the flightdeck. Dodger felt as if it was the condemned man's last walk. In the hanger, three or four others had gathered, and some were donning green hazardous duty lifejackets, one then handed to Dodger. As he put it on, the helicopter started up and the first four were shepherded to the awaiting aircraft. Dodger was last to be seated, next to another armed sentry. The door was rolled shut harshly and locked. The Lynx helicopter now powered up and was soon airborne, soaring up and alongside the speeding warship, then peeling away to starboard, toward distant landfall.

Sixteen minutes later, the Lynx hammered in over the airfield and swooped into land on the helipad. The cabin doors were opened, and six burly men trotted out to the helicopter. They handcuffed the disembarkees as soon as their feet touched the tarmac and lead them away. The Lynx powered up again and lifted off back to *Athene*.

Just over an hour later the mutineers were all ushered toward the steps of a waiting Lockheed Tristar, its engines running noisily. All were now wearing orange overalls and boots, and all were handcuffed. Over the other side of the airfield, several members of the press have gathered behind a cordon and were frantically shooting off photographs and filming.

The prisoners were halted, to wait for the following line to catch up. As they stopped, Dodger turned to Atky.

"I'm shitting myself!" he said, above the noise.

"Me too!" called Atky. Dodger figured it was the first time he'd ever seen Atky afraid, of anything in fact.

An RAF Sergeant appeared out of the aircraft door and signalled for the men to be brought up the steps. As Dodger ascended, he stole a glance over toward the cameras, tracking every move he made. He thought of Louise again, and then his mum and sister. He felt desperately sad, regretful, weary and lonely. On the plane, all mutineers sat across rows with armed guards tending them. The aircraft quickly readied itself, rolled out to the runway and bulldozed along, up and away back to the United Kingdom via Ascension, and the fate of the forty-one, left alive.

Chapter Twenty-Four

Nelson Block, *HMS Rodney*, Portsmouth
16th January 1989
0955

Dodger stood in an echoey corridor in the Discipline Block of the administrative headquarters of the Royal Navy's Portsmouth flotilla. To do so in your best number one uniform with your shoes massively polished meant you were possibly in deep, deep shit … shit so deep you were out of modern sonar detection. At least his uniform was brand new and fitted, as everything else he previously owned was now still in his locker on a trashed Type 42 Destroyer lying on its port side across a rocky plain deep in the South Atlantic. His Naval Lawyer, a Lieutenant Commander Supply Officer had been fair if vaguely unhelpful during the inquiry and charging and Dodger knew a lengthy sentence was imminent. The Officers and Senior Ratings had all backed Fowler as Topsy had predicted and with him now dead and unanswerable to even some of the charges, everything focussed on Dodger. Even Alan Theaker had crumbled under questioning and stitched him up as the main protagonist and guilty bastard of mutiny and likely cause of the deaths of one hundred and six matelots. His shipmates. All those families.

The press had had a fucking field day with him, digging into him and his family and when they found Louise, they hounded her badly throughout the Christmas period with all sorts of bad stories and her ex-es coming out to lather the loofah about 'The Head Mutineer's Girlfriend' including a lurid snap of her topless taken by a boyfriend a few years ago, and further tall, unflattering tales about her personal life and sexual appetite. Before Christmas she ended her relationship with Dodger after a terse, tense and tearful phone call. She wanted to disappear and fast and couldn't do that whilst she was attached to him. It had hit Dodger badly. He didn't want to lose her but could fully understand why she wanted out. Now as he sat there, all he could hear in his head were the words of the Captain of *HMS Emperor*:

"… in the past you have doubted the judgement of certain Commanding Officers in awarding this badge to their prospective Leaders. I certainly hope you give no-one reason to question my judgement when I award this to you. Many people have recommended that you receive this. Their credibility is at stake here. They believe that you have the ability to lead their men and they trust you. I trust you. It's not just a pay rise, MEM Long. This 'fouled anchor' isn't just a badge. It's a lifestyle. People will look, listen and follow your example. You will have influence and knowledge over those below you. They must trust you too. Make sure you read the duties and responsibilities of a Leading Hand before you sew on these badges. Understand them, young man …"

Opposite Dodger was a door. A temporary sign on it said, "Court Martial in progress."

The handle on the door turned slowly and the door inched open. It stayed like that for around twenty seconds, and distant voices could be heard from within. Then it sharply swung open fully.

"LMEM LONG!" shouted a voice from within the room.

"Sir" answered Dodger and snapped to attention.

Dodger was led into the room by the Leading Hand, followed in turn by an Officer. The door banged firmly shut behind them.

1336

Dodger slowly and sullenly walked along the upper walkway of Royal Naval Detention Quarters adjacent to *HMS Rodney*. He entered the cell one from the end and stood before the bunk. Sunlight shafted down through the small window, ten feet from the floor. He was now dressed in service No 8 clothing minus the fouled anchors and carrying blankets and a pillow. The guard slammed the door shut behind him with a bang. This was his home tonight until his transfer to civilian prison the day after tomorrow.

Chapter Twenty-Five

Westcroft's DIY Store, Portsmouth
Wednesday, November 29th, 1989
1302

Fowler is at the counter and has a headache. The assistant whose name apparently was Pauline and was 'Happy to Help' was a late-middle-aged woman and very, if not overly cheerful. Well, she was for Fowler.

"That'll be eight-seventy-five, please," said Pauline, and Fowler paid with a crisp, ten-pound note. He waited patiently for his change. He was unkempt, unshaven by four days and scruffy. He placed the three-inch diameter length of hosepipe into the large Westcroft-logoed carrier bag and exited the shop, not even thanking Pauline.

*   *   *

The inquiry had been bad for practically everyone. Independent investigators were brought in from all corners of the government departments and compiled and studied testimonies and transcripts of what happened. Of the survivors in the life rafts, only one or two managed to escape with small blemishes on their records, the rest had reprimands and sanctions which either finished, or at best limited individual careers. Of the surviving twenty-one mutineers on *Warwick*, all were either punished with custodial sentences, serious fines or issued with 'Service No Longer Required' orders, effectively a sacking and they were promptly booted out.

Further up the line the Squadron Flag Officer was reappointed elsewhere along with other senior staffers and the First Sea Lord was effectively relegated to a lower post. The new First Sea Lord came crashing in and issued a series of commands to mete out the highest penalties as an example to all. Thatcher's own Defence Secretary, very wobbly in his own previously comfy position, had a torrid time in the Commons against massive calls from all sides and even the right-leaning broadsheets for him to resign over the matter. And then the tabloid press, famished from decent scandal for some time descended on the main characters and picked the bones clean. Fowler's marriage was disassembled. Colleen Fowler gave her own story to the News of the World in exchange for £350,000 and Topsy's distraught and blameless family, hailing from hard-bitten, working-class Burnage in Manchester, were pursued relentlessly regardless of the fact that their dead and guilty son and brother had been a main protagonist in a major military incident, resulting in the deaths of over one hundred of the nation's sons and the loss of a key government military asset worth £350m to the taxpayer. John Fisher's widow was still pursuing the Daily Express through court for libel and defamation as they had named him as one of the main ringleaders, and other families had to move schools and neighbourhoods. At the pinnacle of all this however stood a Junior Rating, still alive, now contemplating prison and infamy. Two teenage children of two separate now-dead members of *Warwick*'s ship's staff had attempted suicide and Naval Family Support Services were more overwhelmed than they were during the higher tension phases of the Falklands Crisis seven years prior to this. The Royal Navy struggled badly to figure out how to keep the victims' families from disappearing under the surface of a murky lake of individual crisis. The shockwaves rippled out and shook everything, sometimes to the point of collapse.

Fowler made a desperate case against the mutineers and in particular Dodger as he presented them all as a main protagonists. The Board of Inquiry, headed by a Rear-Admiral and containing a Royal Marines Colonel, several legal entities and a bastion of opinion formers as advisors tried vainly to remain independent and objective but suffered two staff changes itself and huge internal disagreements. Fowler's behaviour leading up to the mutiny was the main plank of Dodger's case and was reinforced by corroborating accounts from the mutineers and, key to the case, two of *Warwick*'s own senior Officers. The manslaughter of Doc Savage and the people on the Flight Deck, the murders of Harry Wilmott and Jon Fisher all remained on file for further investigation and charges. The BOI just needed to know how the mutiny happened and who made it happen and if the acts were illegal. After sixty-two days of consideration and deliberation during which the mutineers all remained under close arrest and confined to barracks (one escaped and was still at large, believed out of the country) the findings were submitted and charges framed. The whole process in

Dodger's instance would be transferred to civilian Crown Court, the trial beginning at the Old Bailey in March of 1989 and to complete by that May. Dodger faced charges with conspiracy to commit mutiny against the Crown under the Mutiny Act 1873, itself carrying the death penalty as the maximum tariff and this was still actually extant, but not possible due to the abolition of the death penalty superseded fortunately by the Naval Discipline Act of 1957 and abolition under the Human Rights Act.

Mick and Atky, plus three other surviving Leading Hands were charged at military Courts Martial with a lesser crime of failure to suppress a Mutiny. A handful of gun-carrying Able Seamen close to Topsy also had this charge levelled against them, whilst most others escaped with reprimands and summary punishments and/or fines plus loss of Good Conduct stripes if applicable. Some of these were discharged the Service.

The only person to walk away from the incident unscathed was Petty Officer Simon Crawford, who was drafted at his own request out of the Portsmouth area and took his story through eight years more service, stoically never mentioning a word about it to anyone, particularly executing Topsy Turner, the main mutineer.

With everyone punished effectively and justice seen to be done, the Royal Navy hoped the story would stop dripping when further wrung out and everyone would drop it and move on.

Lt Cdr Patrick Fowler Royal Navy faced a severe reprimand, which effectively halted his career and was offered a convenient exit door out of the service which, after some quiet advice from a senior officer or two he reluctantly took, retaining his pension rights and benefits and his rank upon leaving. His last day in the service was coincidentally the same day Dodger was transferred to Winchester Prison to start his fifteen-year sentence.

*   *   *

Thursday, November 30th, 1989

0730

The postman spritely bounded to the door next to Fowler's and delivered the mail through the letter box. Somewhere in the background a car engine was running, and he hoped he could catch the occupant before they left for work because they had a registered letter that needed a signature of receipt. He came through Fowler's front gate and initially passed the car with the engine ticking over, and as it was a chilly day he assumed the driver was just warming it up. He gave it a cursory glance and carried on delivering the mail.

As he came back past the car, he slowed to look through the window. He was startled by what he saw and yanked at the door which was locked. He went round to the passenger side and tried the door. It was also locked. He straightened up, looking round desperately, but there was no other person around at that time in the morning. Again, he looked through the glass. Fowler was reclined in his driver's seat amongst the blue smoke of the car's exhaust. His face was grey and he was obviously quite dead. On the windscreen, in the condensation was written, "NO MORE!"

Wednesday, May 6th, 1998
C wing, Long Fenton Prison.
0930

Dodger is sat on a metal bench with another prisoner, Tex. Both are smoking. They are casually watching other prisoners playing Uckers down below on the lower landing. One of them calls out, "Hay-thang-you!" and taps his counters round the board and Dodger smiles knowingly. Somewhere, *Brimful of Asha* by Cornershop is playing on a radio.

"Time is it, shippers?" asked Tex.

"Half nine," said Dodger. "He's fucking late. I'll sue."

Tex lifted his arse off the bench and stared down to the far end of the wing above the Uckers players. "Hold up," he said. "Looks like he's here."

At the far end of the lower landing, the security door opened. Three suited men and two screws emerged, one of the suits looked up at the balcony, spotting Dodger, smiling. Dodger rose, smiled back and waved. Tex got up, putting his cigarette into his mouth and offered Dodger his hand.

"David 'Dodger' Long," he said. "Last of the Warwick Mutineers. See you then, you lucky, six throwing, timber-shifting twat!"

Dodger's eyes welled up with tears. It hadn't been a particularly tough time inside for him, but now hopefully he could walk free and get on with his life. Outside was a changed world, his mum had died four years ago from a stroke and according to his sister, Louise had married, had a daughter and then divorced. Anything could happen, he hoped, quietly.

"Yeah!" said Dodger and both men hugged hard. "Stay in touch, eh?"

"You bet!" Tex gasped a bit. "Write me when you get sorted out, eh?"

Dodger took his cigarettes out of his pocket and gave them to Tex. "Here," he said. "I've just given up."

Tex accepted them. "Stay out of trouble. Or you'll be fucking needing them. Shipmate."

Dodger chuckled, wiping away a tear. "Sure. Bye then!" He turned, picked up his bag and trotted off along the landing, down the stairs and toward the suits.

AFTERWORD

This book came to me as follows:

Circa May 1994, *HMS Newcastle*,
Joint Maritime Course, North Sea
Machinery Control Room, First Watch

LMEM 'Jessie' James: "Slinger, we were having a discussion earlier down the mess. Do you think us killicks and the lads could run this ship on our own?"

PO 'Slinger' Woods: *(thinks a bit)* "What? Y'mean, no Chiefs, POs or Officers?"

LMEM 'Jessie' James: "Yeah. Like, just us. Fight a war. Go into action. That sort of shit. Take the ship over and run it."

PO 'Slinger' Woods: "Like … get rid of us? How? Like say … a mutiny?"

Printed in Great Britain
by Amazon

95d6baec-0e39-45ba-85fa-2e47d4d40398R01